BAD BABY

ROSS MacDONALD

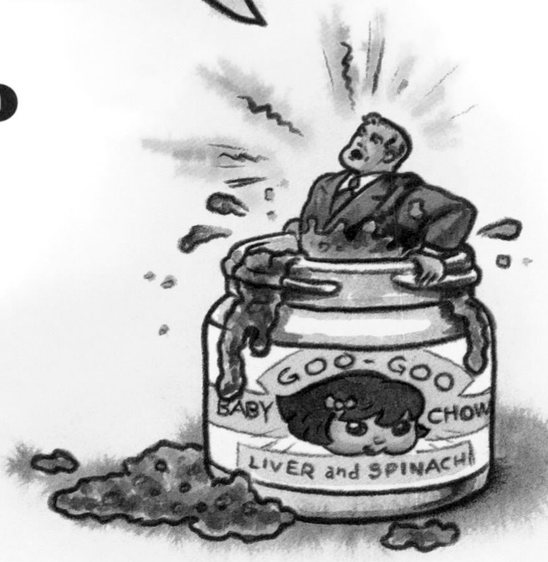
GOO-GOO
BABY
CHOW
LIVER and SPINACH

A NEAL PORTER BOOK
ROARING BROOK PRESS
NEW MILFORD, CONNECTICUT

For Lucy and Jamie and especially Daisy

Copyright © 2005 by Ross MacDonald

A Neal Porter Book

Published by Roaring Brook Press

Roaring Brook Press is a division of Holtzbrinck Publishing Holdings Limited Partnership

143 West Street, New Milford, Connecticut 06776

Distributed in Canada by H. B. Fenn and Company Ltd.

Library of Congress Cataloging-in-Publication Data

MacDonald, Ross.

Bad baby / Ross MacDonald.— 1st ed.

p. cm.

"A Neal Porter Book."

Summary: Superhero Jack finds his life turned upside down
by the arrival of a very big, and very naughty, baby sister.

ISBN 1-59643-064-8

[1. Brothers and sisters—Fiction. 2. Babies—Fiction. 3. Heroes—Fiction. 4. Play—Fiction.] I. Title.

PZ7.M1513Bad 2005   [E]—dc22   2004024454

Roaring Brook Press books are available for special promotions and premiums.
For details contact: Director of Special Markets, Holtzbrinck Publishers.

First edition September 2005

Printed in the United States of America

2 4 6 8 10 9 7 5 3 1

Jack was having another perfect day.

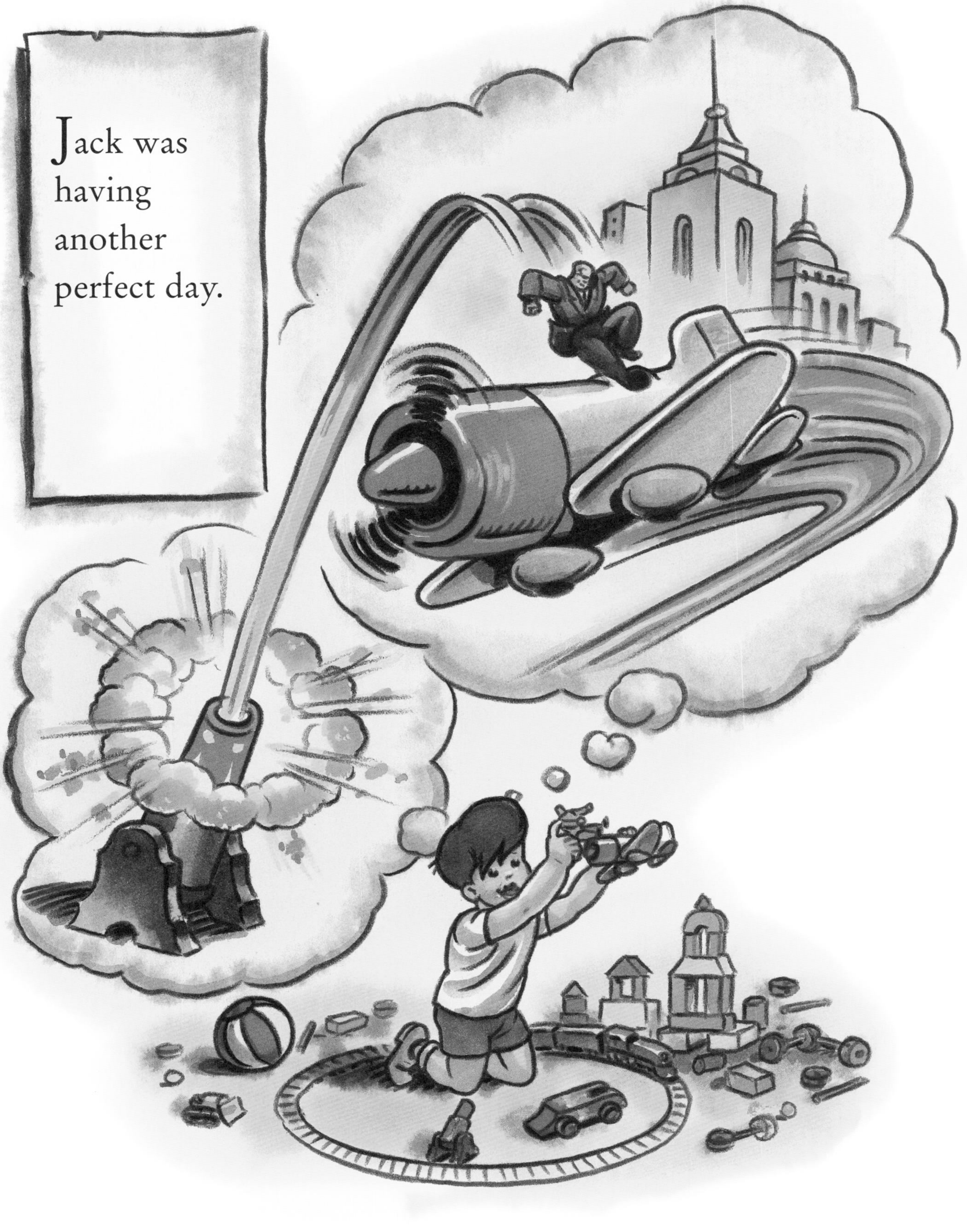

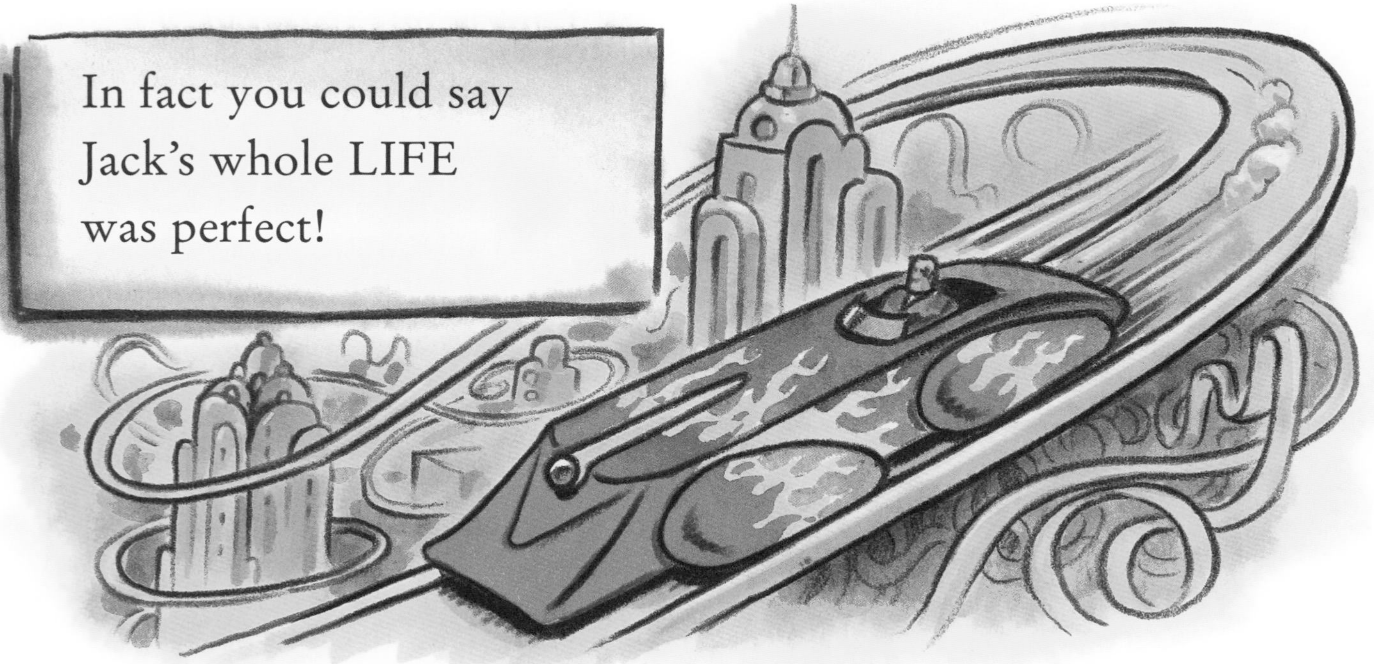
In fact you could say
Jack's whole LIFE
was perfect!

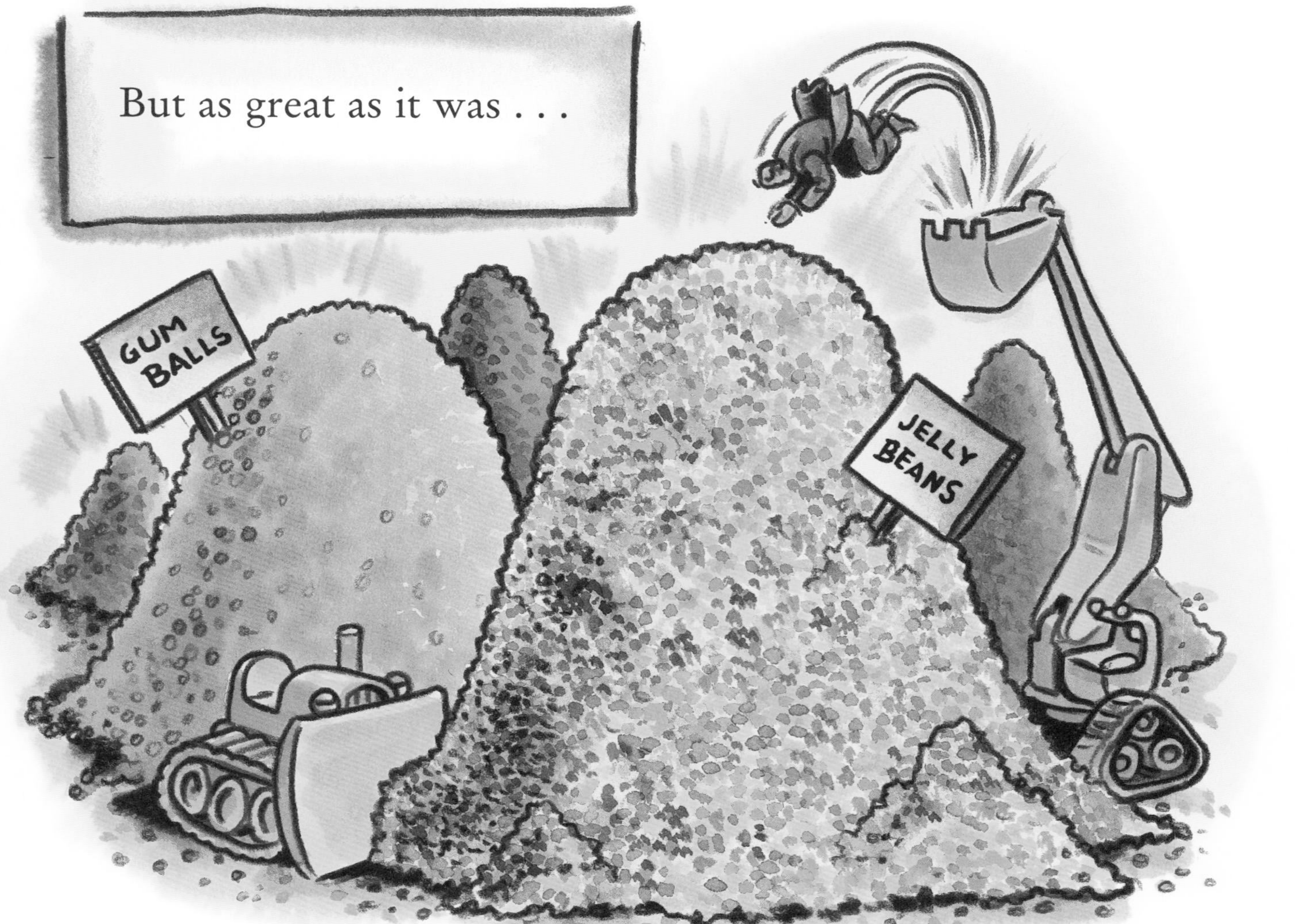
But as great as it was . . .
GUM BALLS
JELLY BEANS

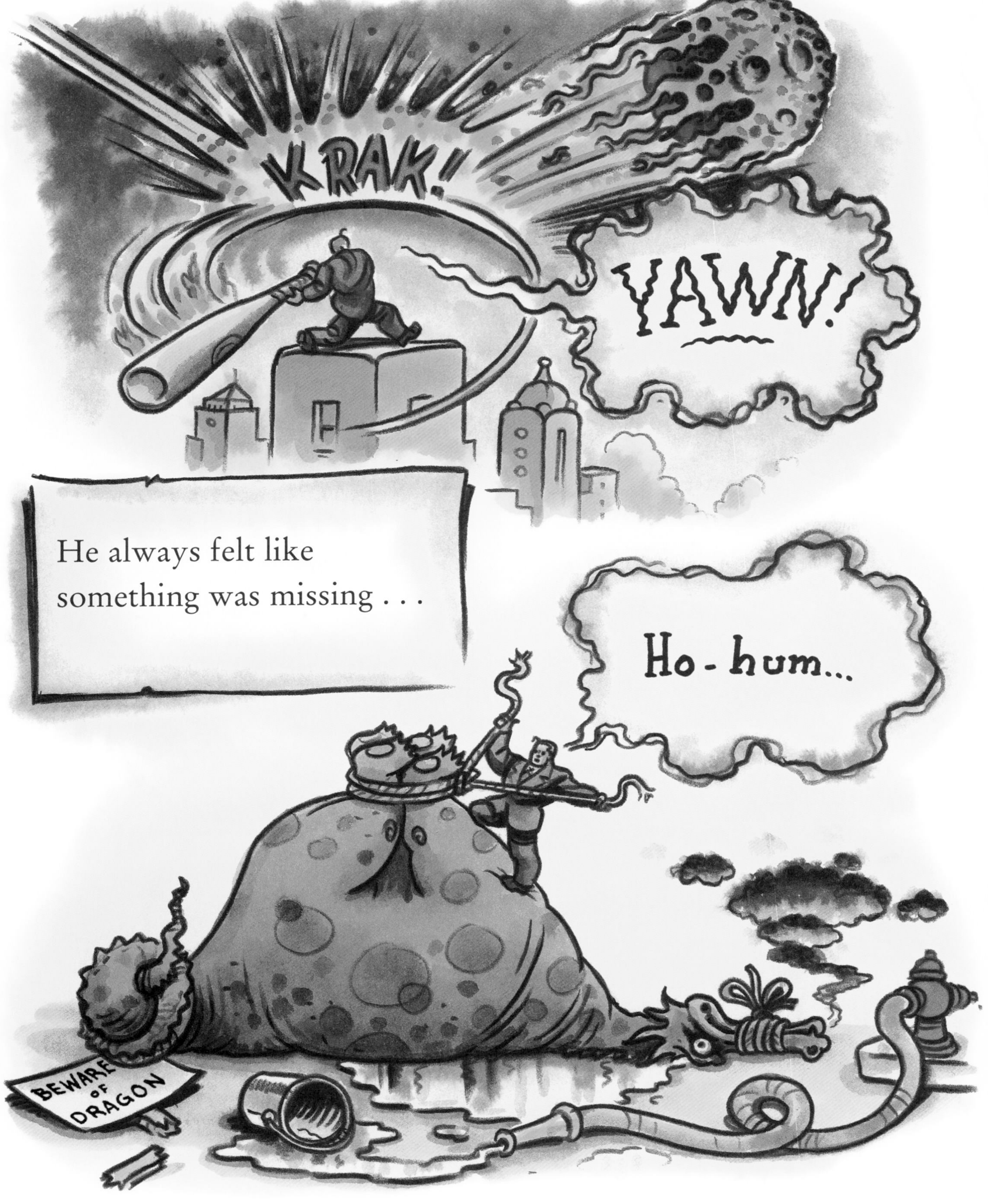
KRAK!
YAWN!
He always felt like something was missing . . .
Ho-hum...
BEWARE OF DRAGON

But what
could it be?

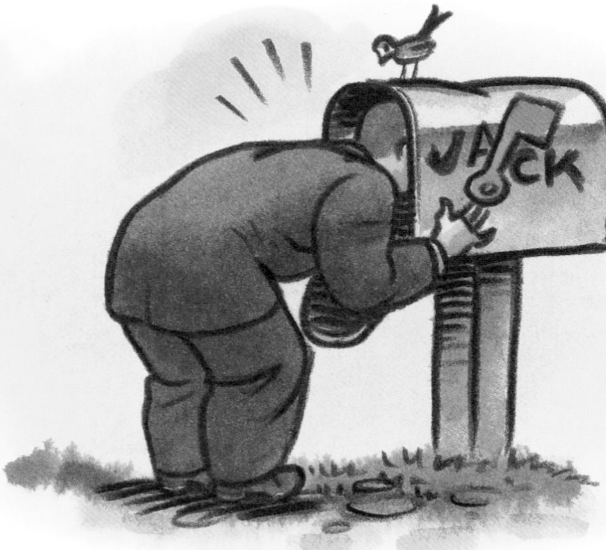
JACK

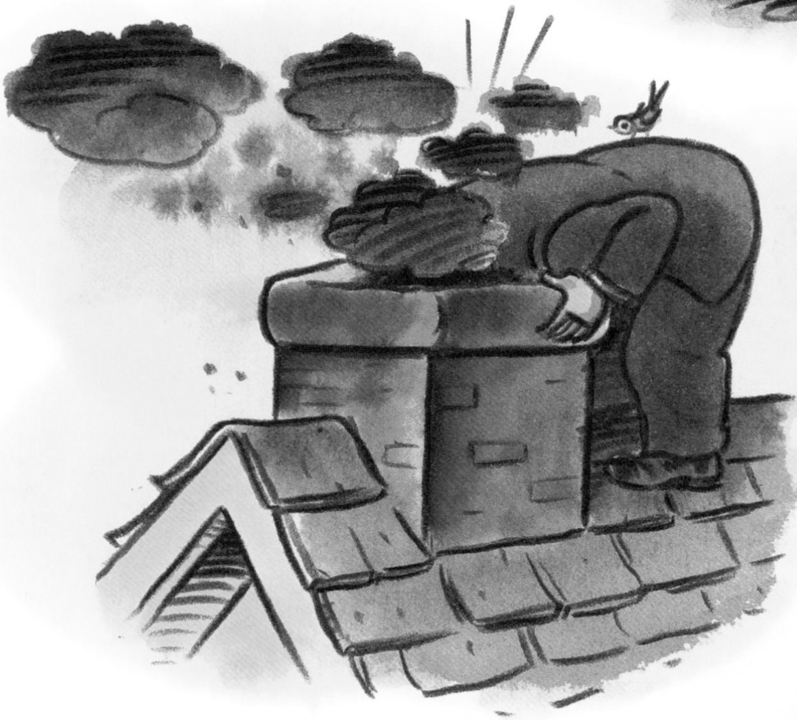

Jack looked
high . . .

and low.

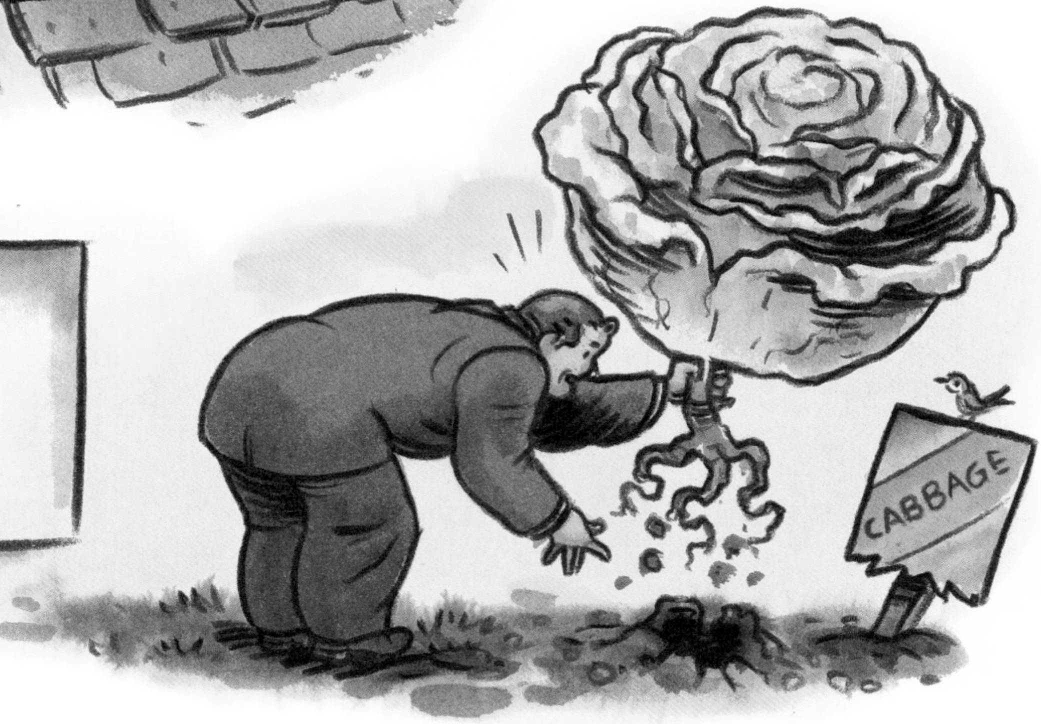
CABBAGE

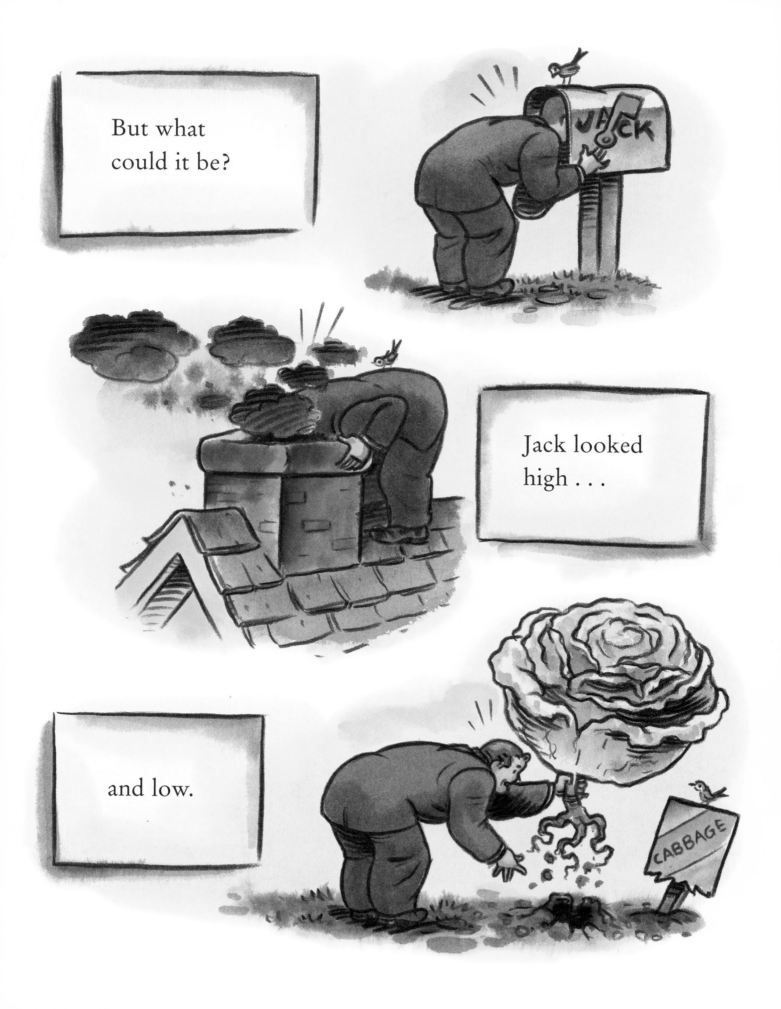

Then one day he heard the great news—
he was getting a new baby sister!

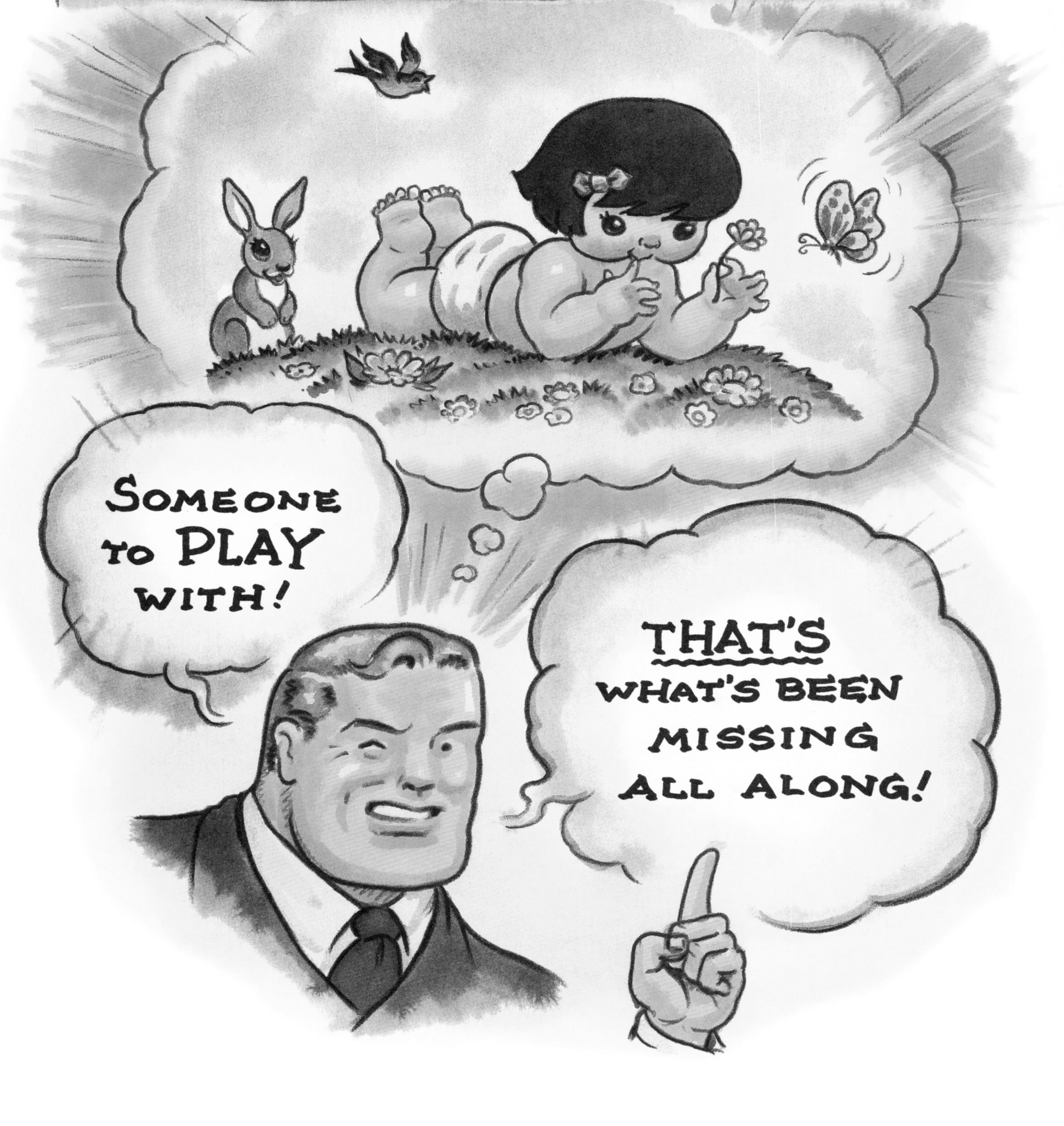
SOMEONE TO PLAY WITH!
THAT'S WHAT'S BEEN MISSING ALL ALONG!

When she first came home she was so little and cute, he called her

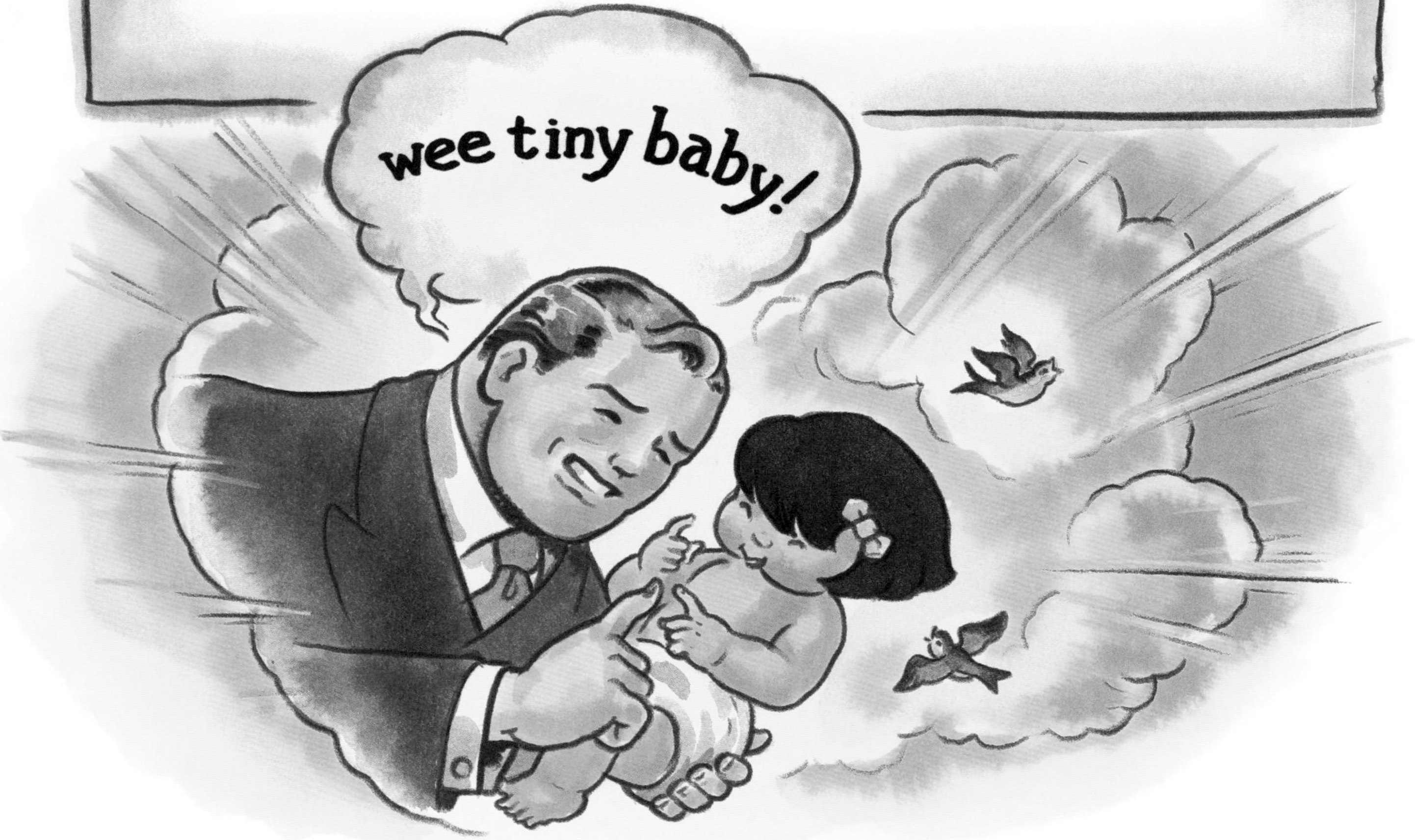
wee tiny baby!

But she grew . . .

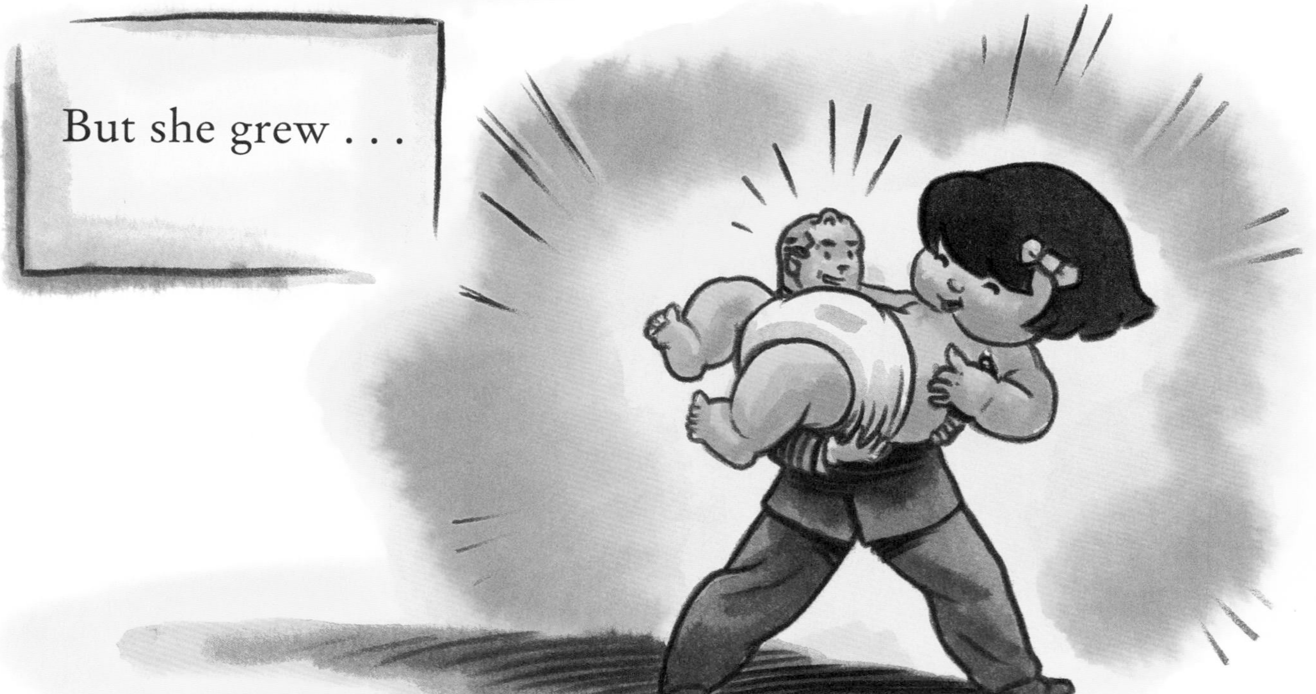

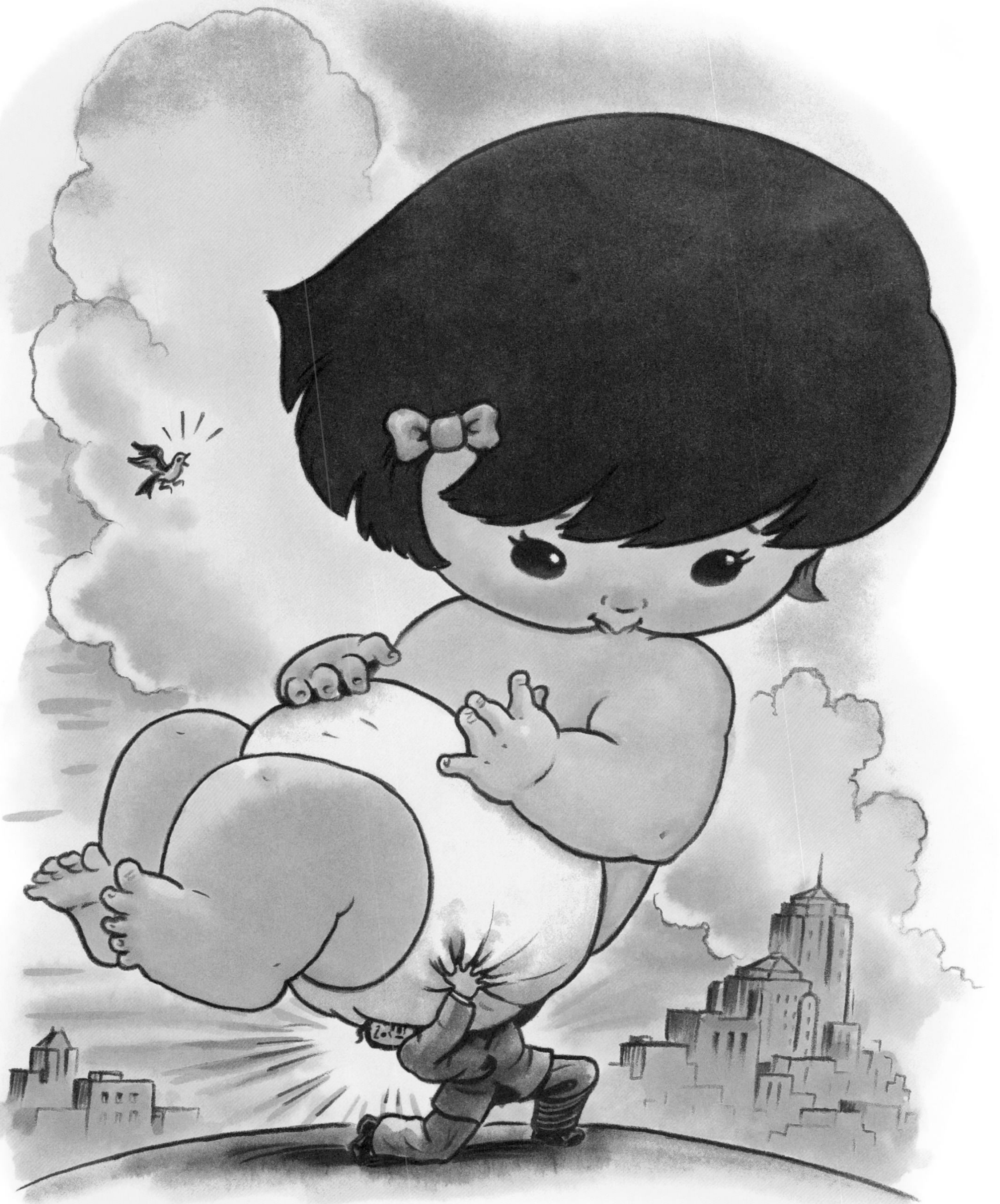

And GREW!

And soon she was walking,

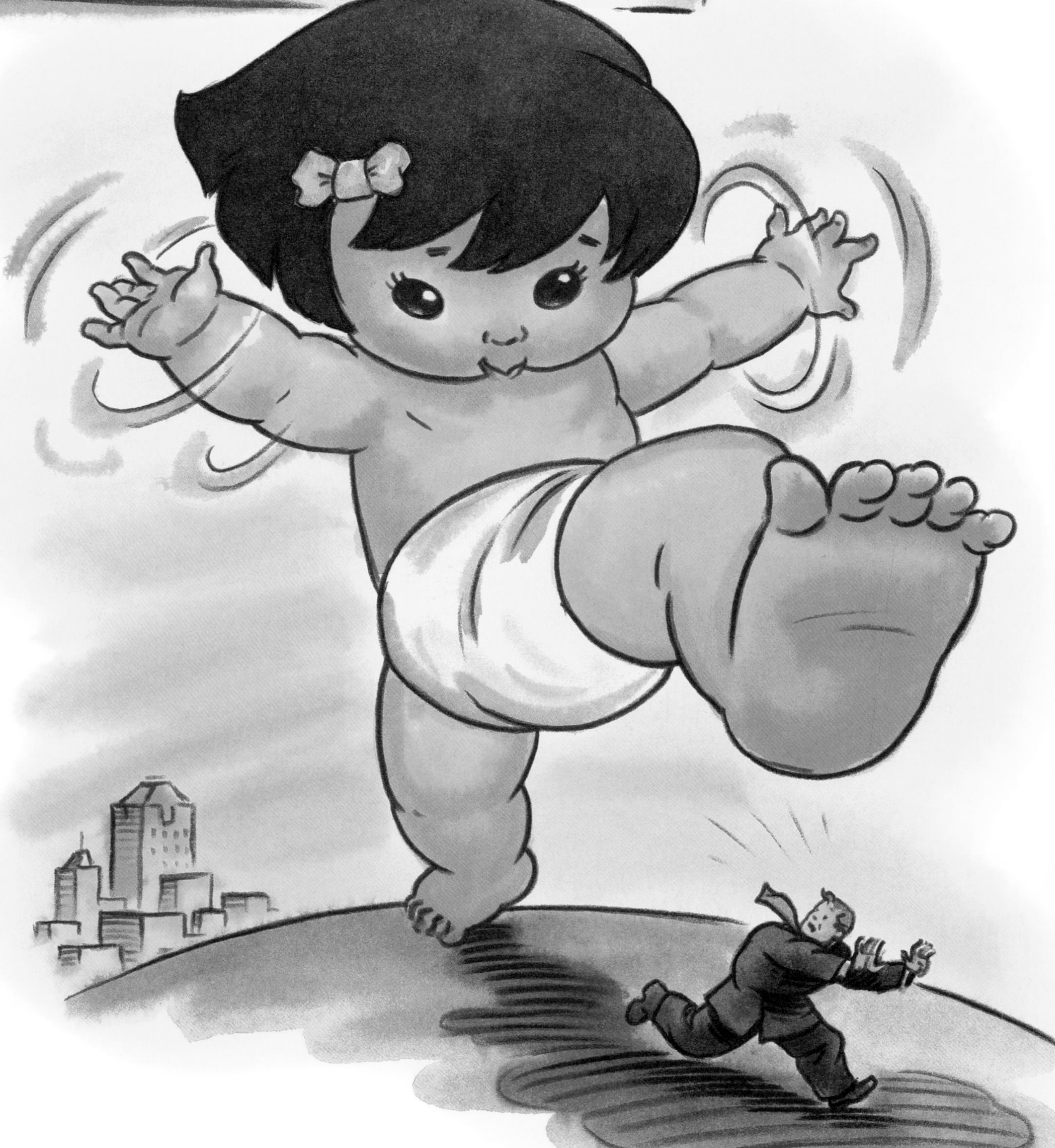

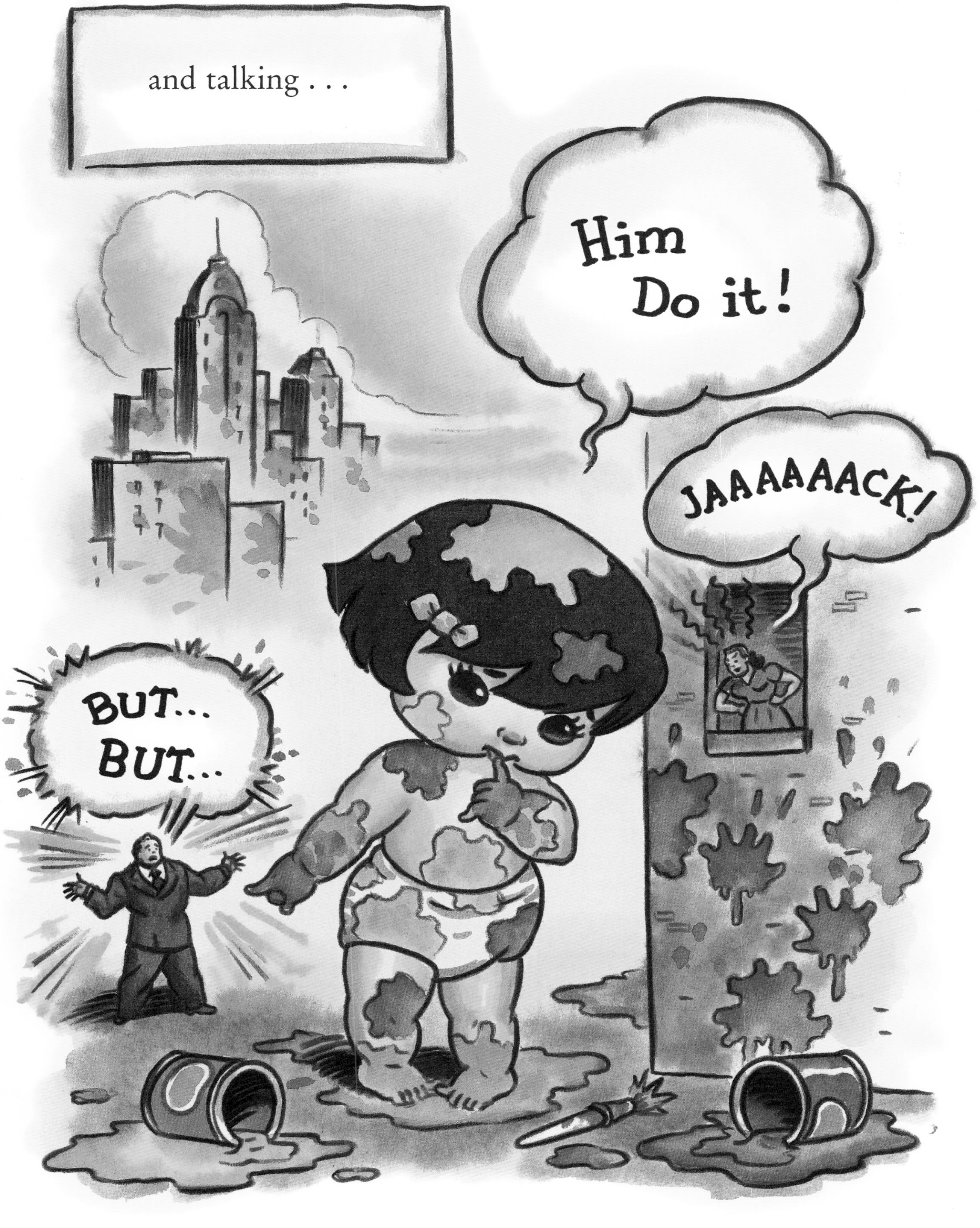
and talking . . .
Him Do it!
JAAAAAACK!
BUT... BUT...

And doing all kinds of ADORABLE things . . .
like playing peek-a-

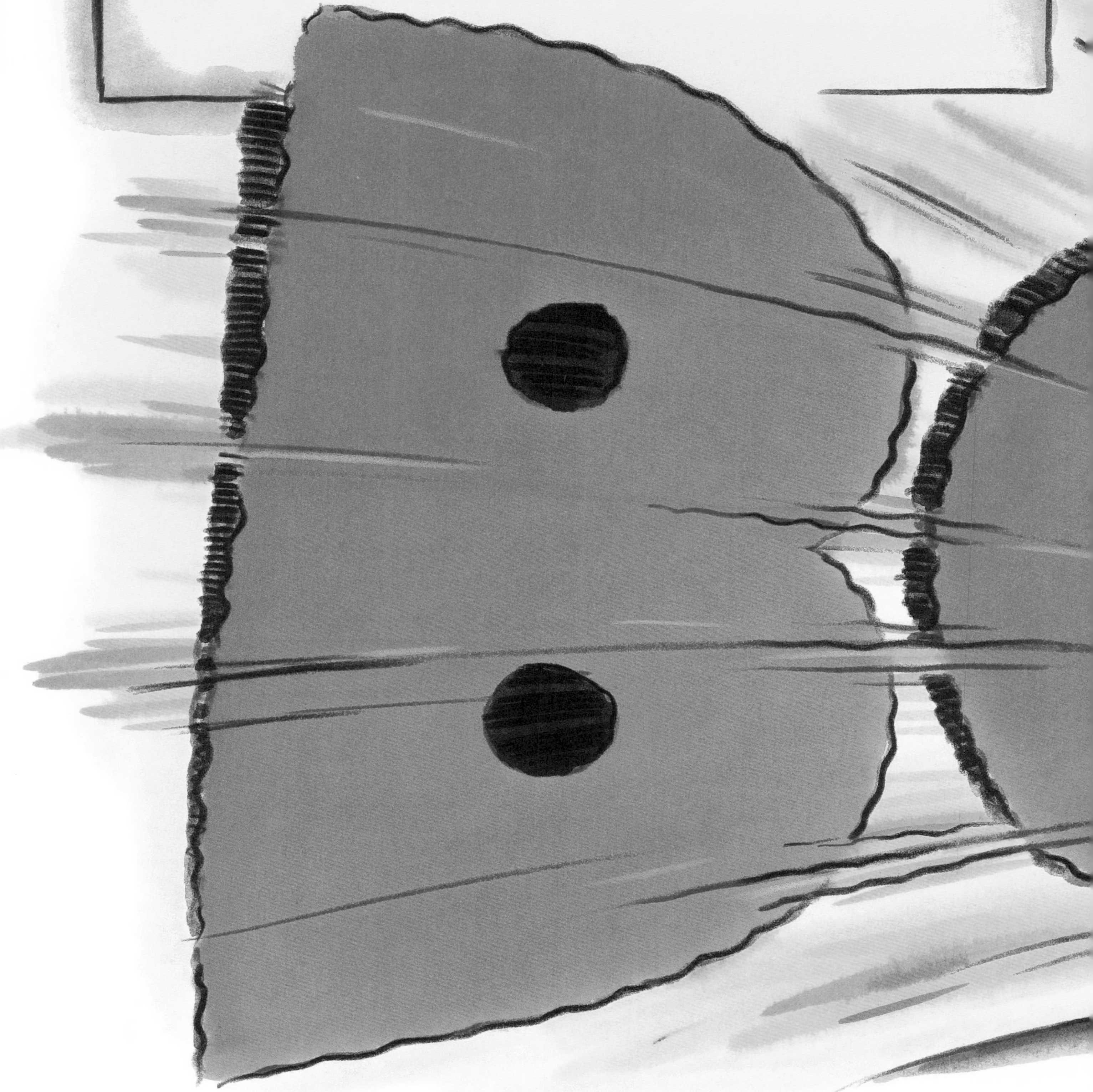

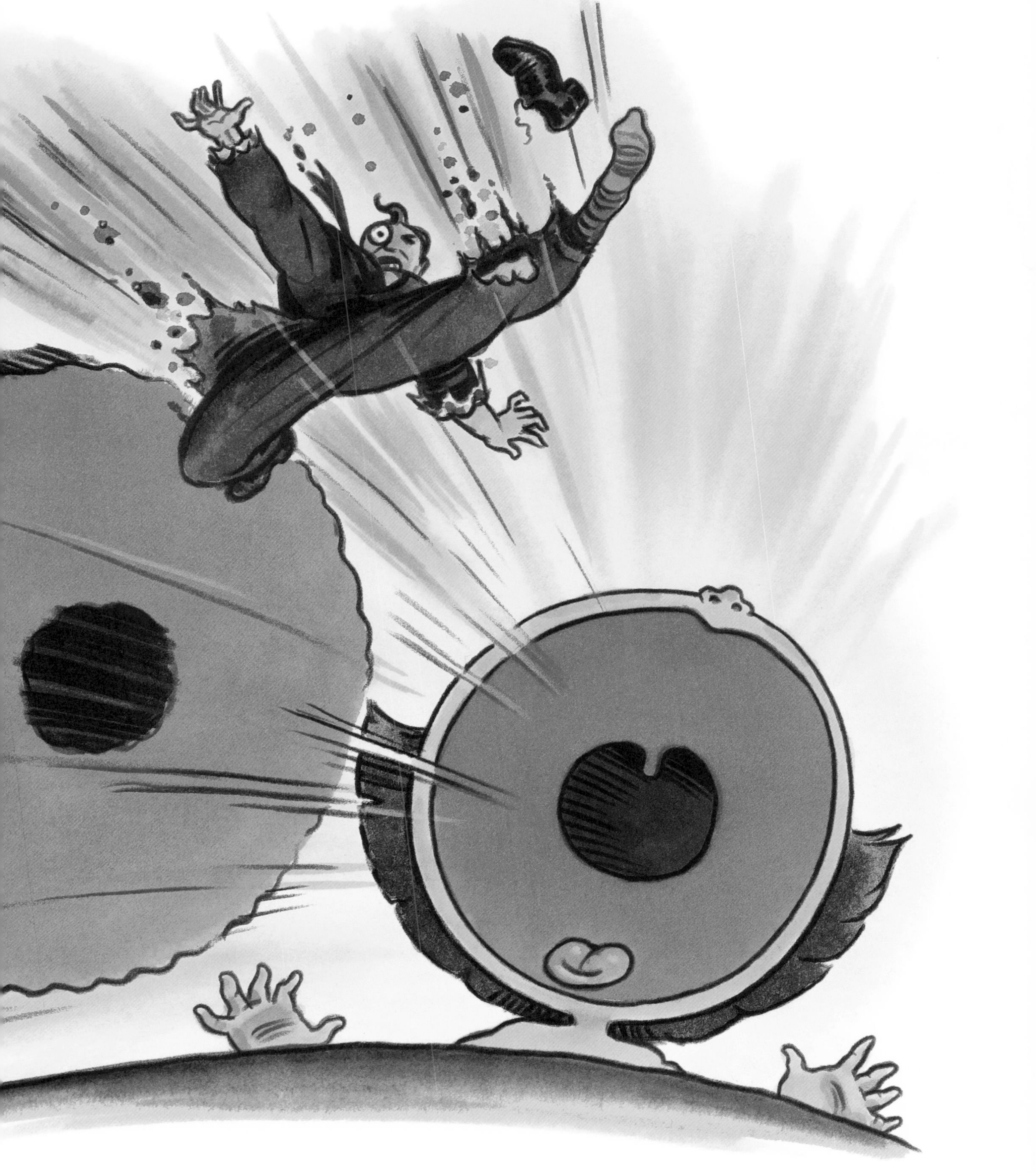

And tag.

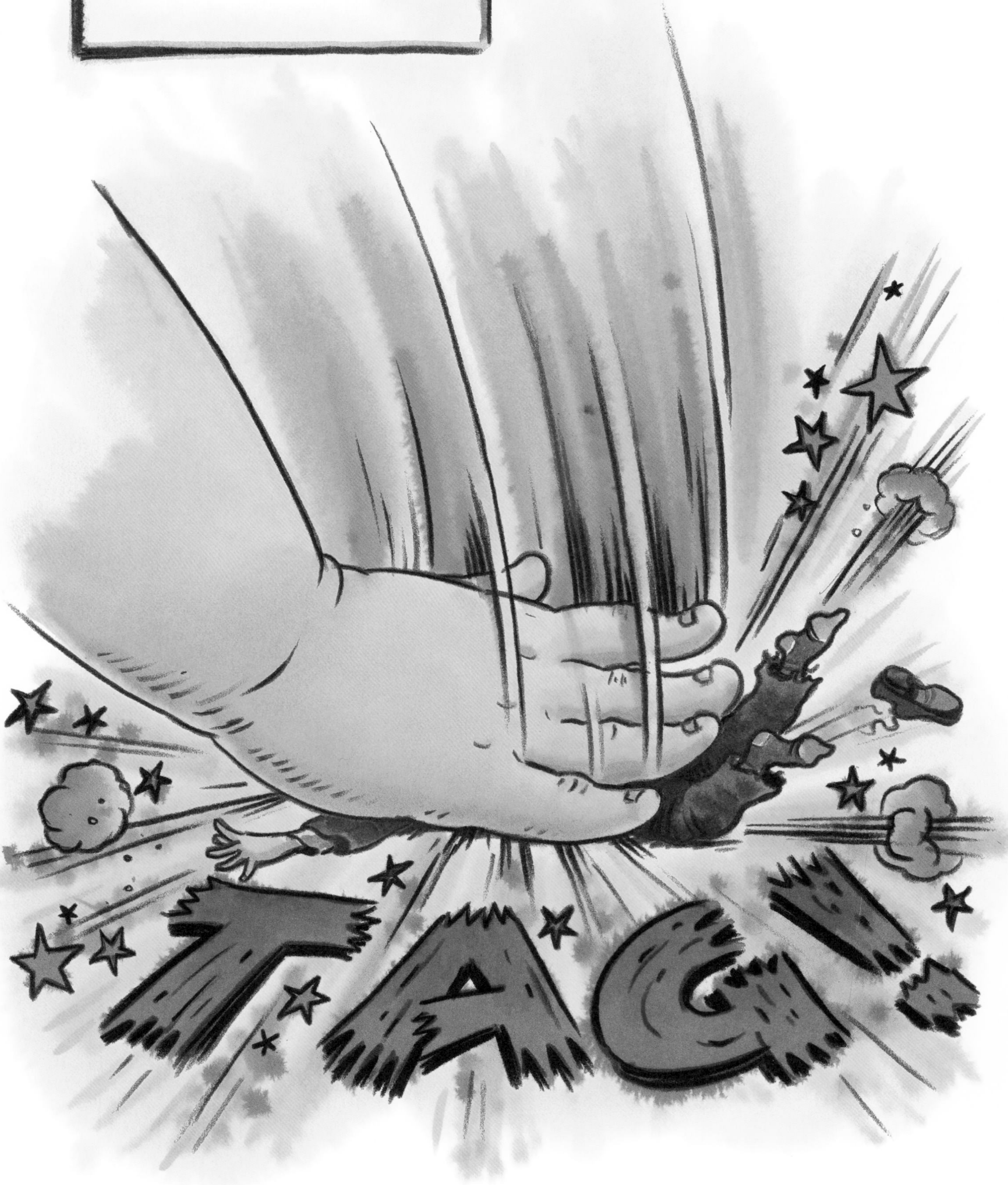
TAG!

Having tea parties . . .

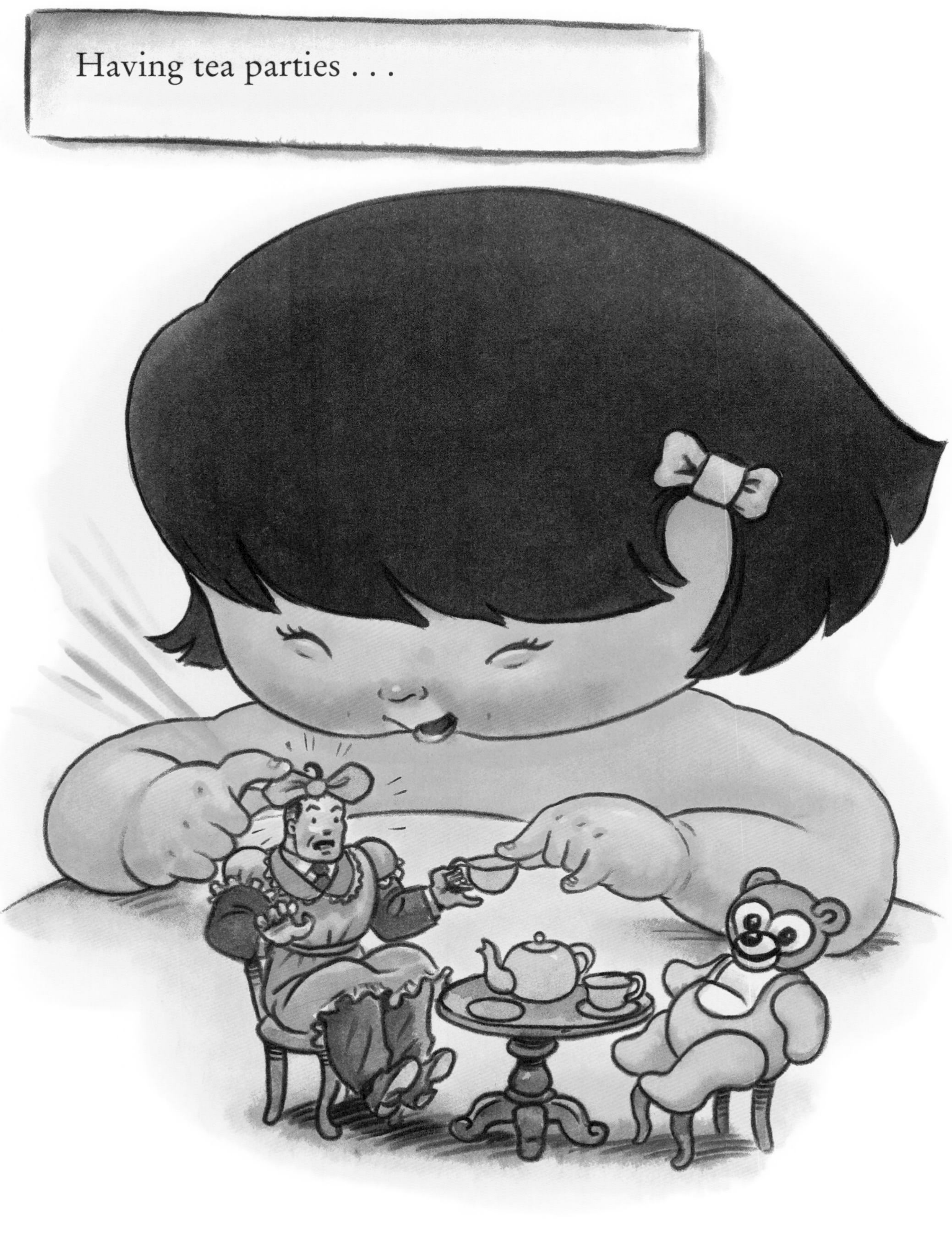

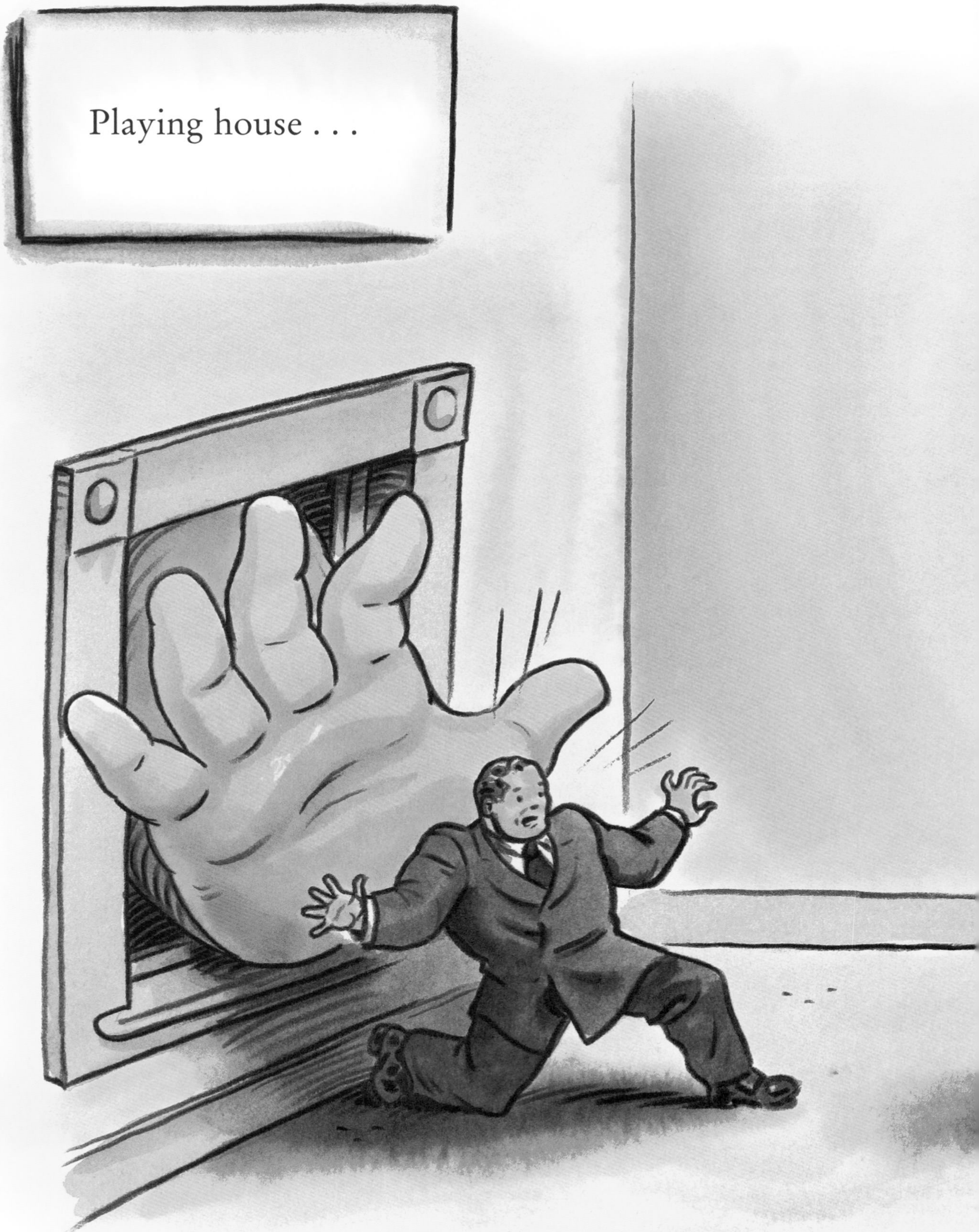
Playing house . . .

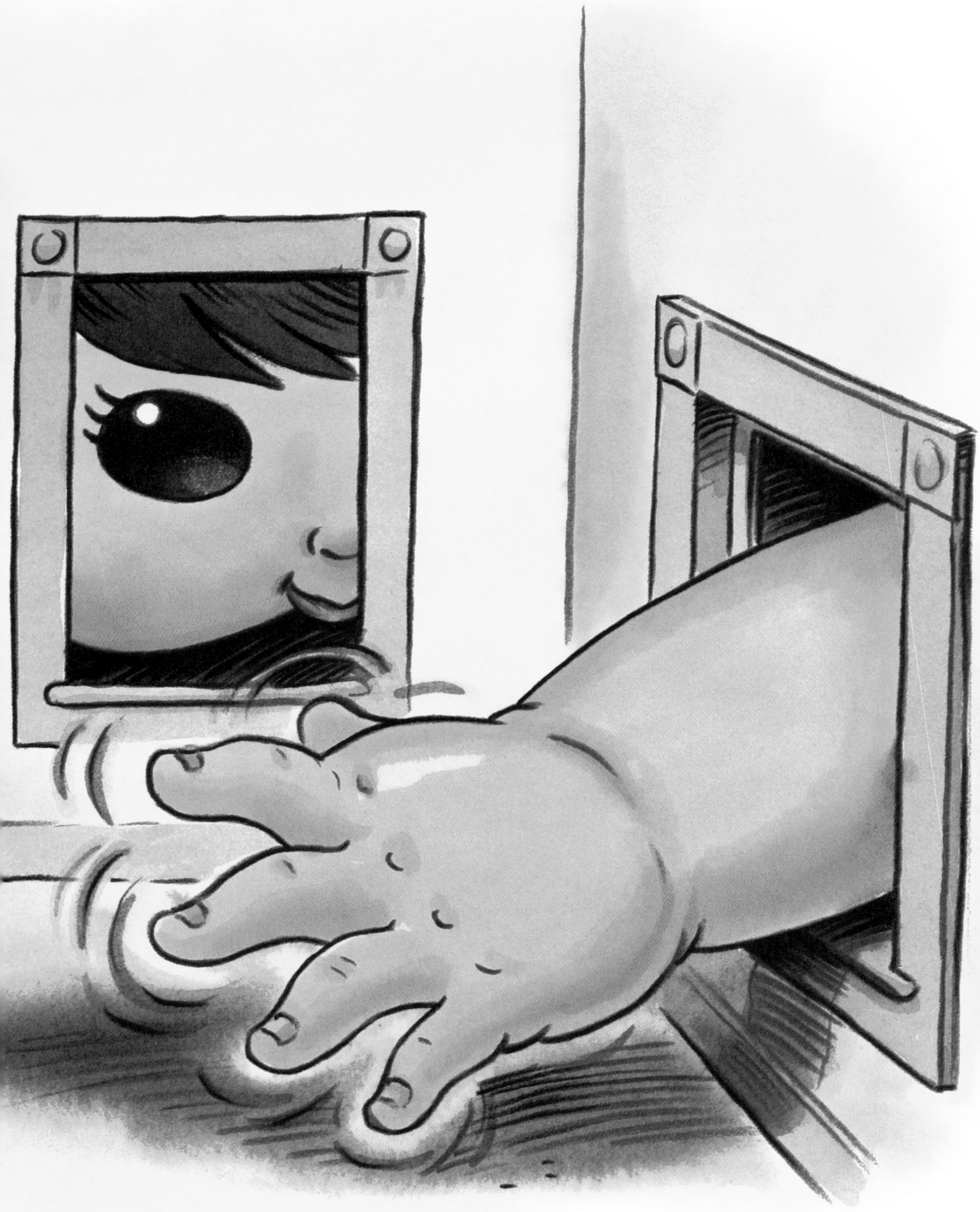

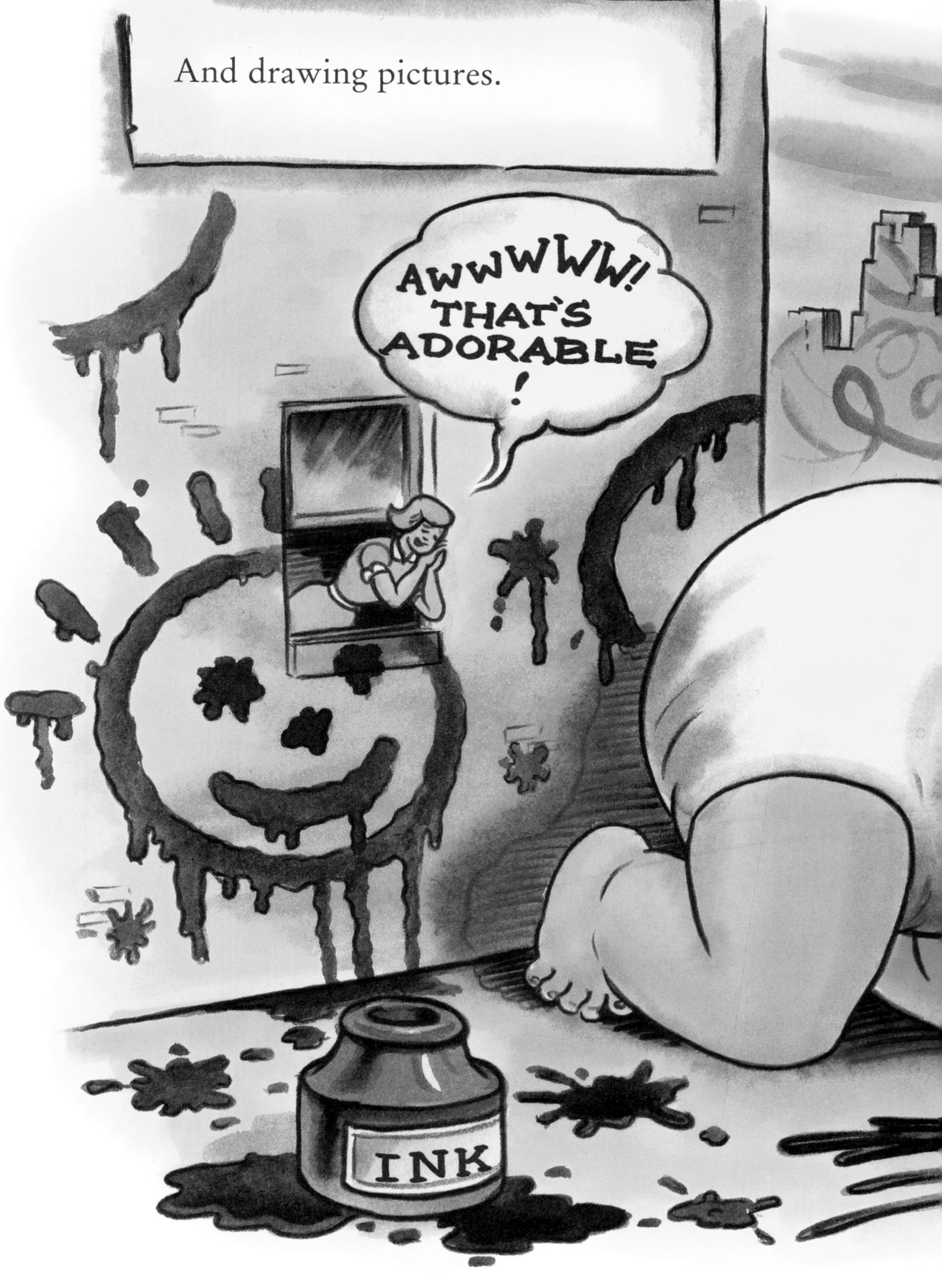
And drawing pictures.
AWWWWW! THAT'S ADORABLE!
INK

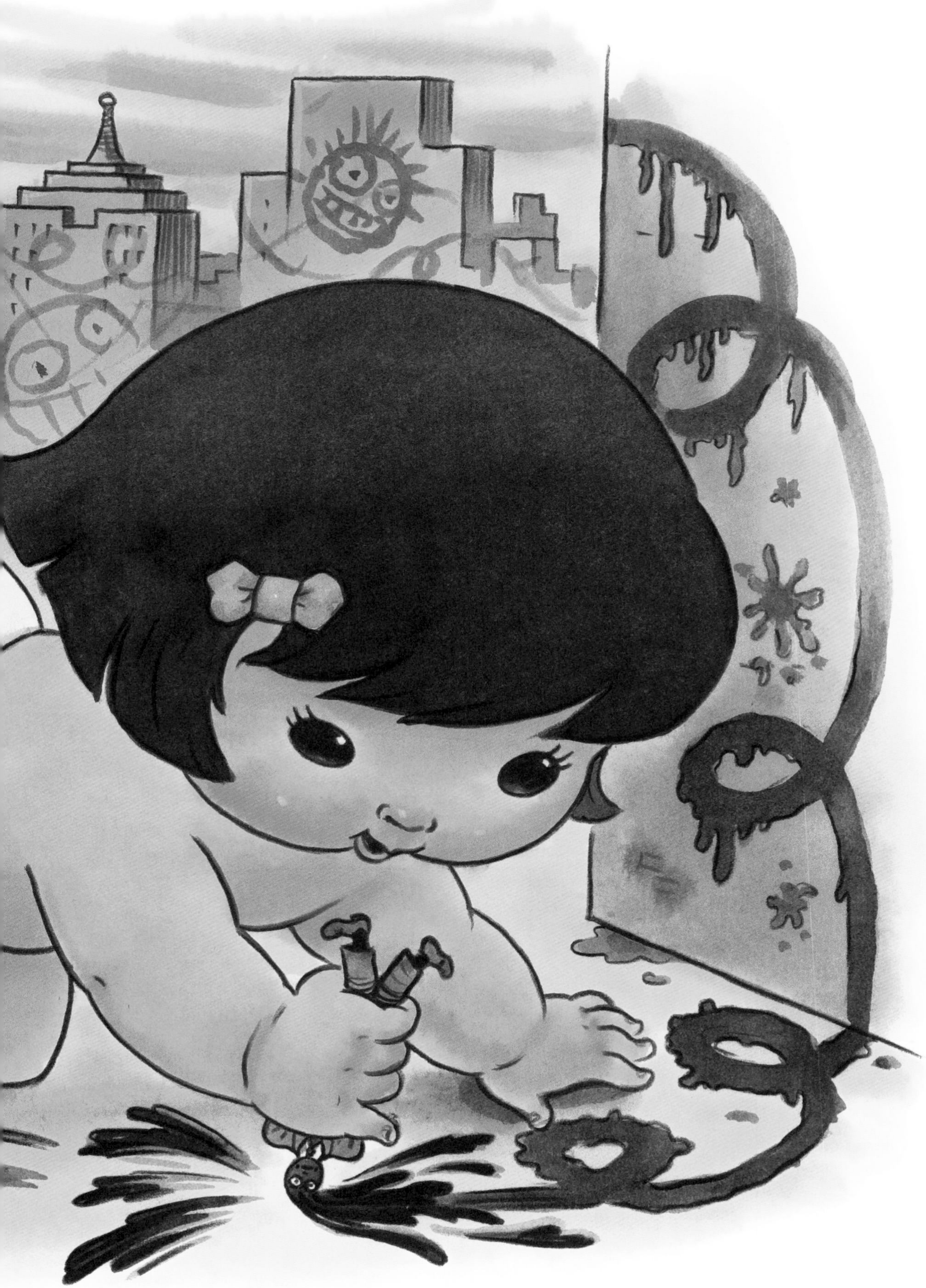

She liked to share her lunch . . .

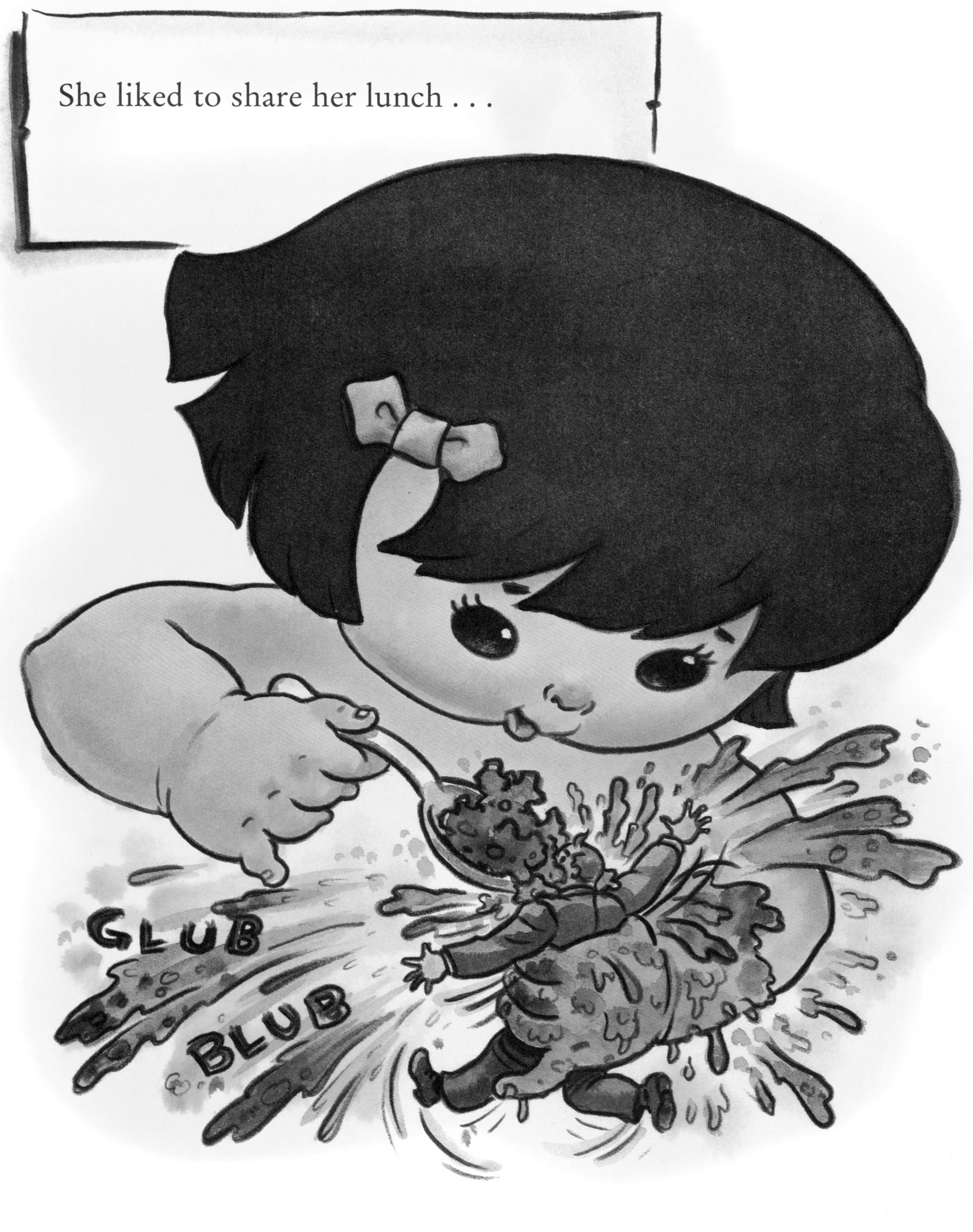
GLUB
BLUB

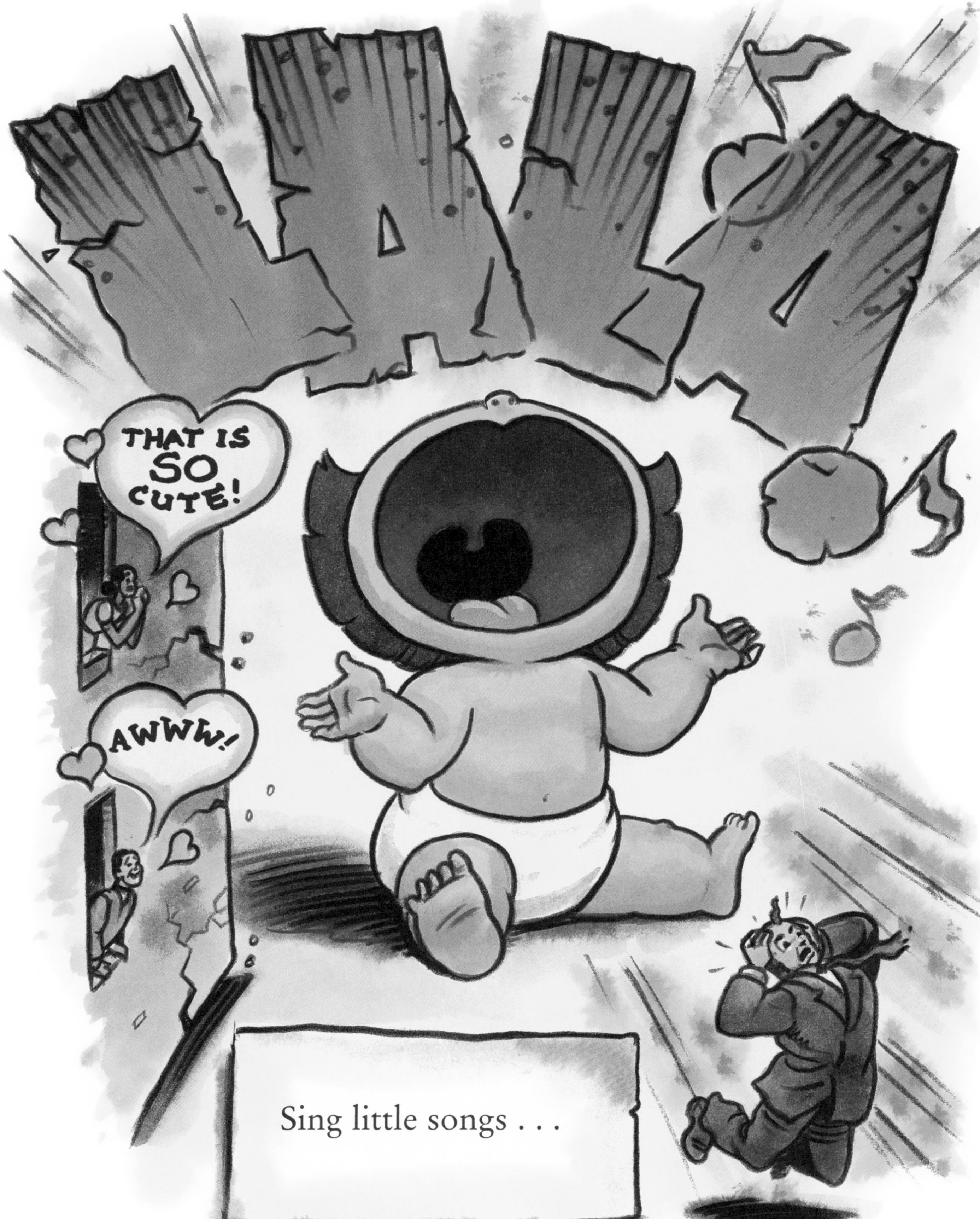
LALA
THAT IS SO CUTE!
AWWW!

Sing little songs . . .

And play with Jack's toys!

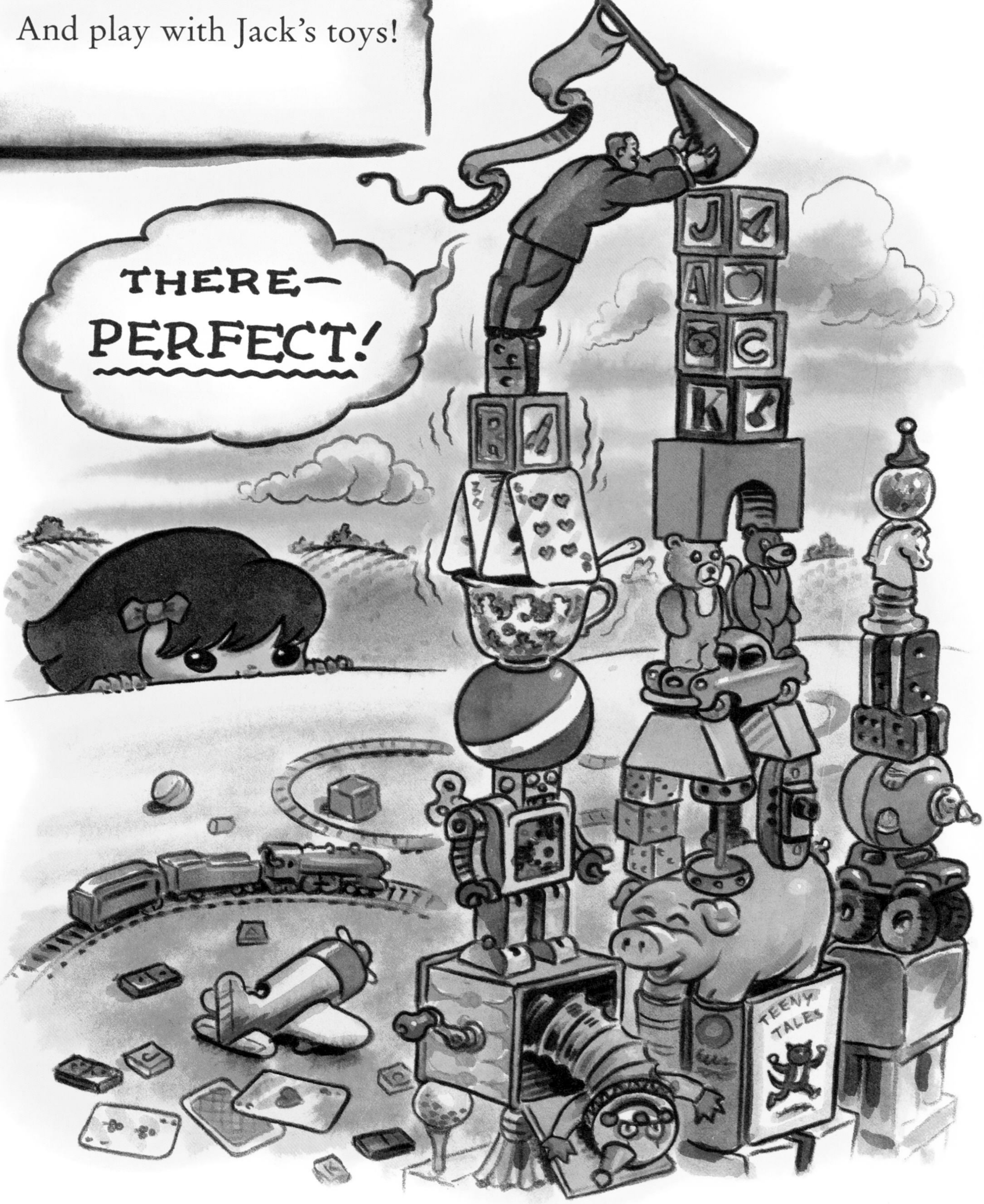
THERE—
PERFECT!
TEENY TALES

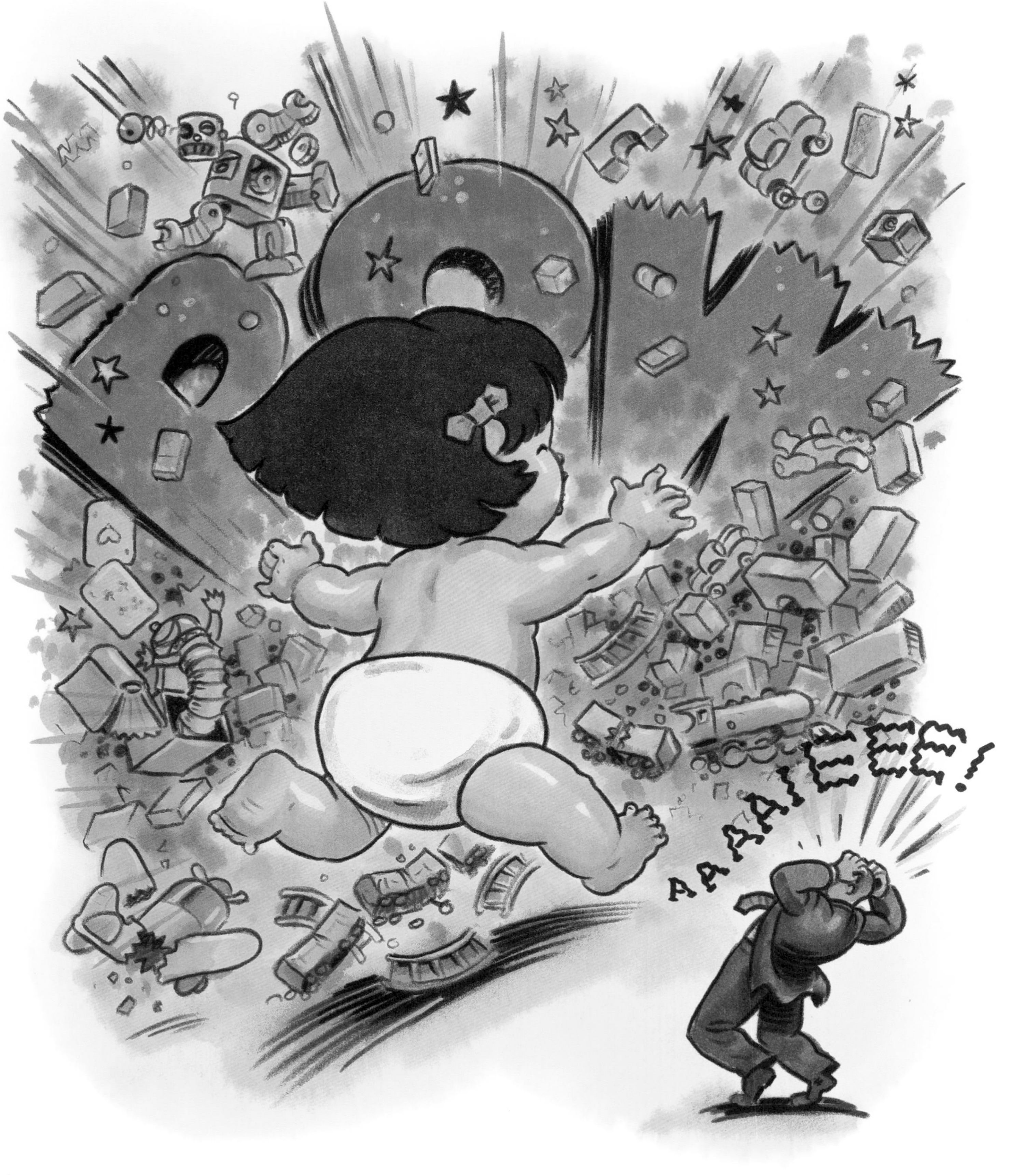
AAAAIEEE!

But she wasn't ALL play—no! She also liked to pitch in and help with the dishes,

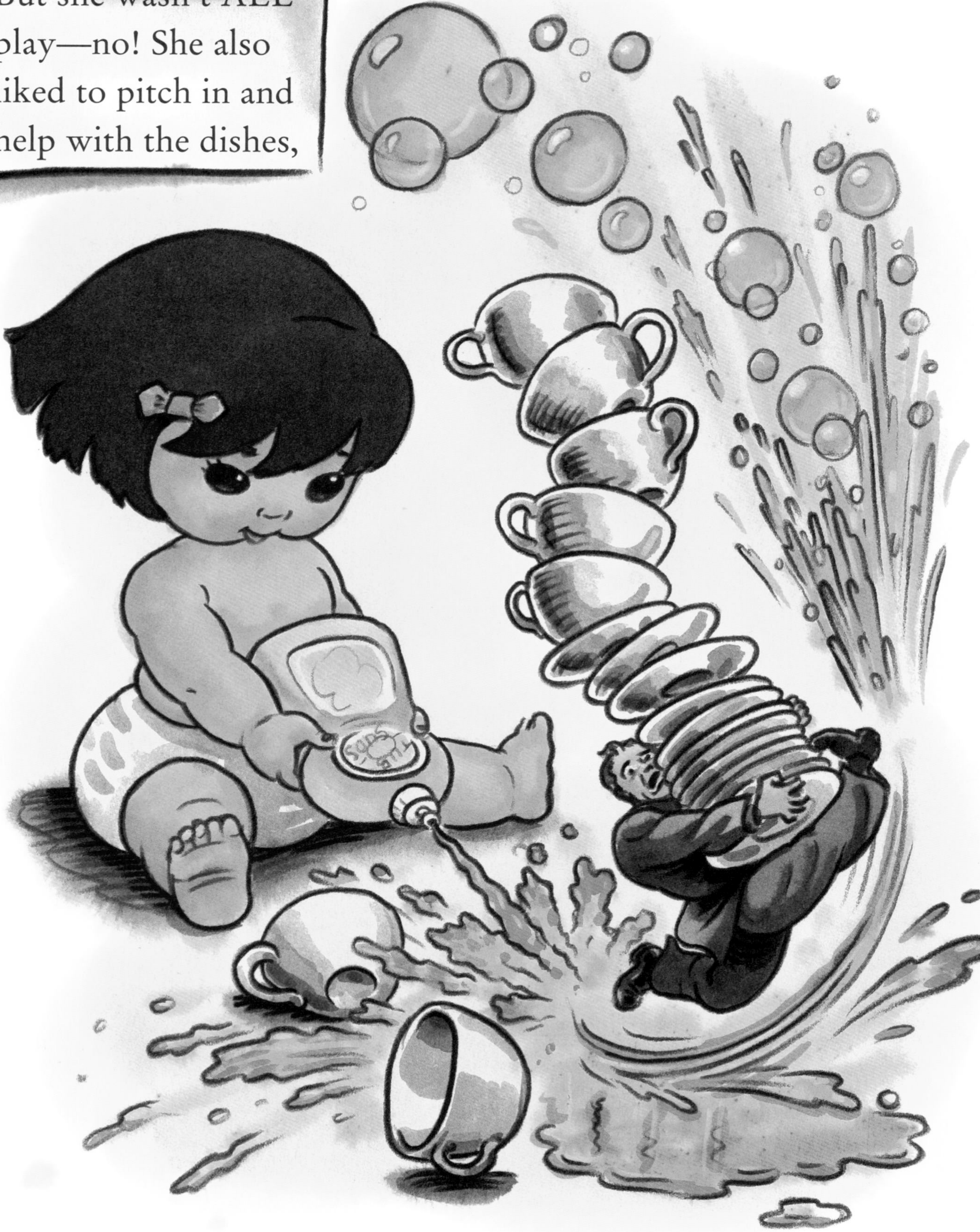

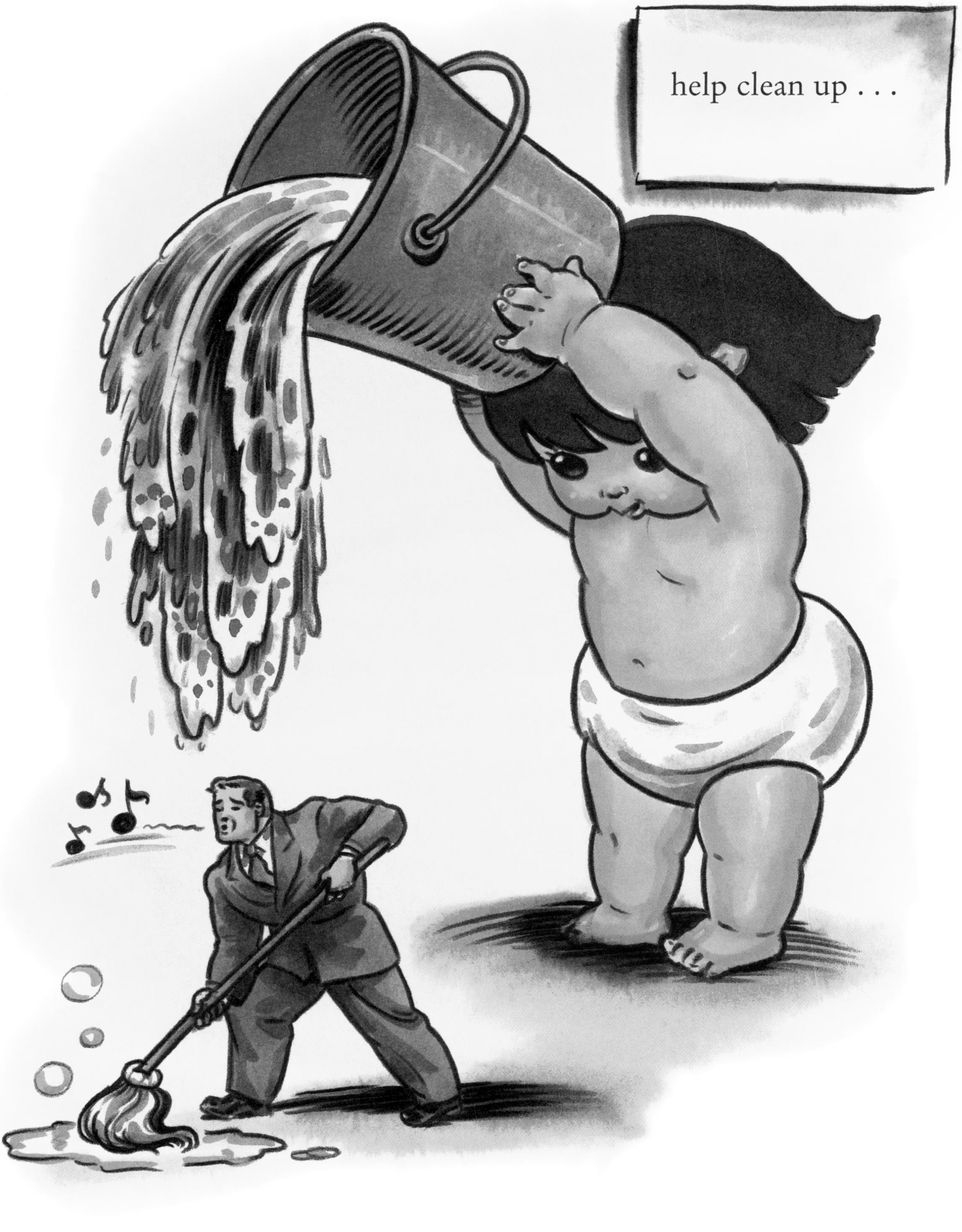
help clean up . . .

And help make the beds.

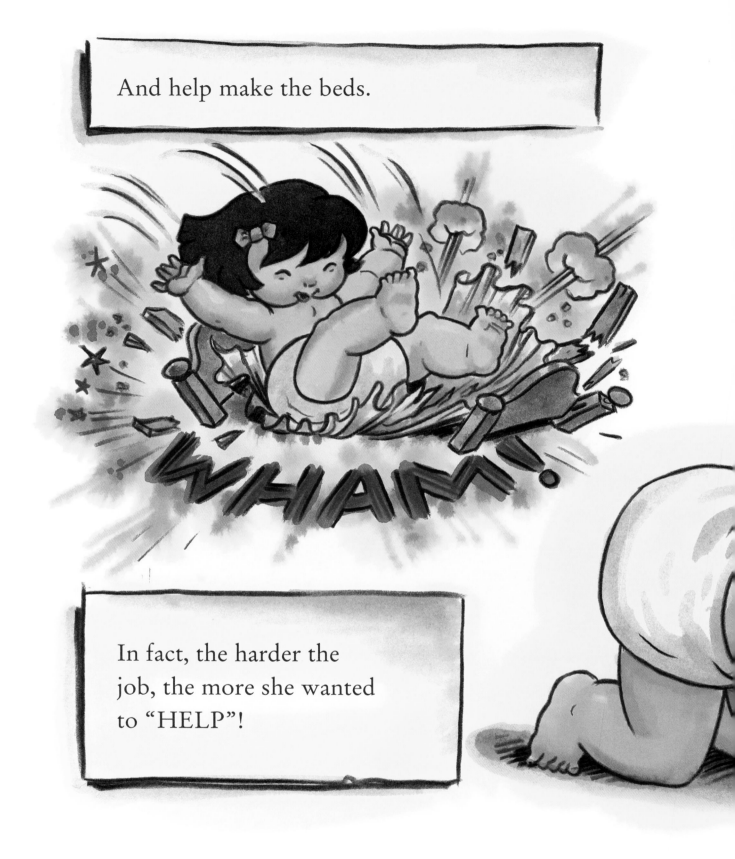

In fact, the harder the job, the more she wanted to "HELP"!

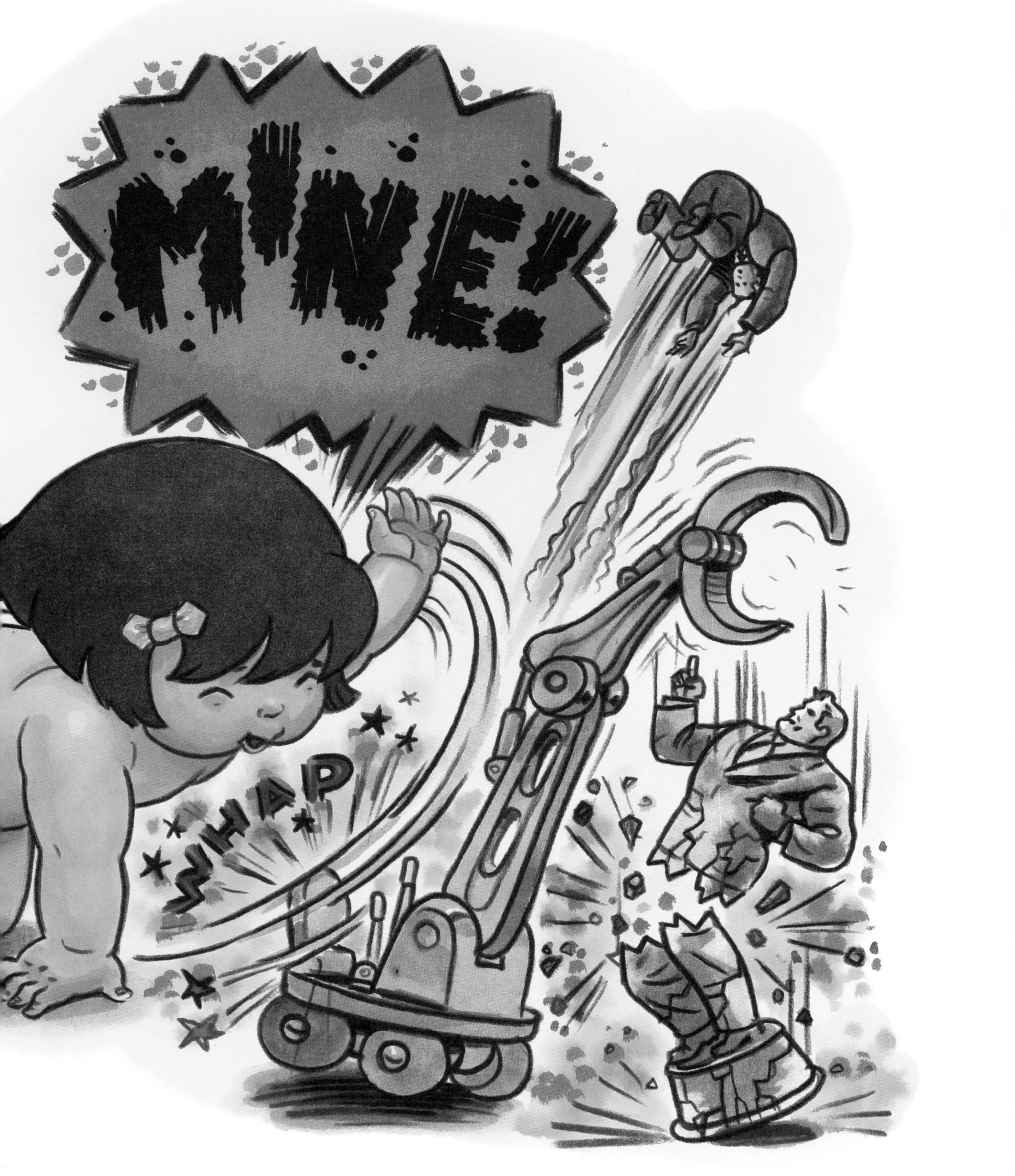
MINE!
SHAP

She loved her big brother Jack.

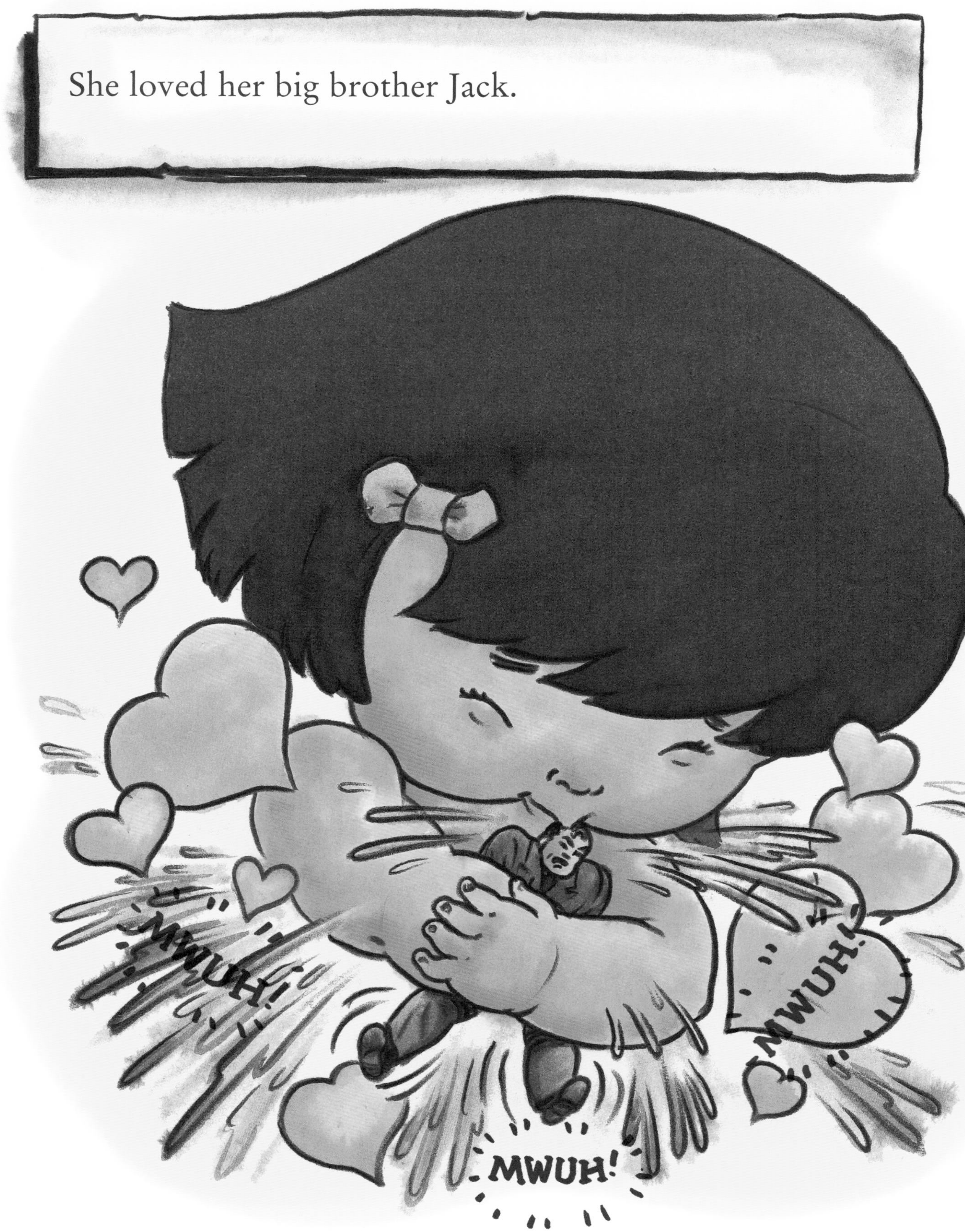
MWUH!
MWUH!
MWUH!

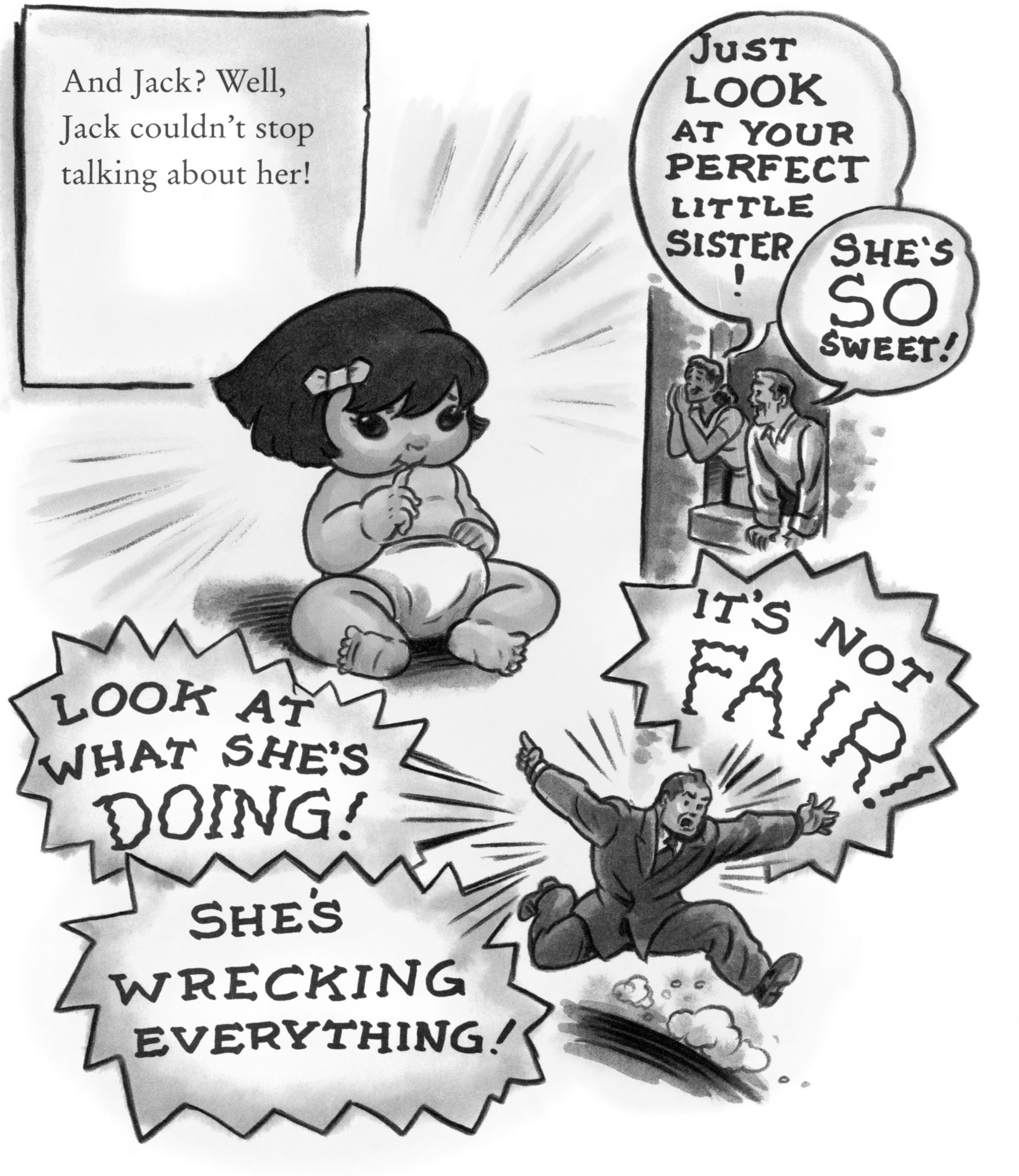
And Jack? Well, Jack couldn't stop talking about her!
JUST LOOK AT YOUR PERFECT LITTLE SISTER!
SHE'S SO SWEET!
LOOK AT WHAT SHE'S DOING!
IT'S NOT FAIR!!
SHE'S WRECKING EVERYTHING!

He loved seeing her first thing in the morning . . .

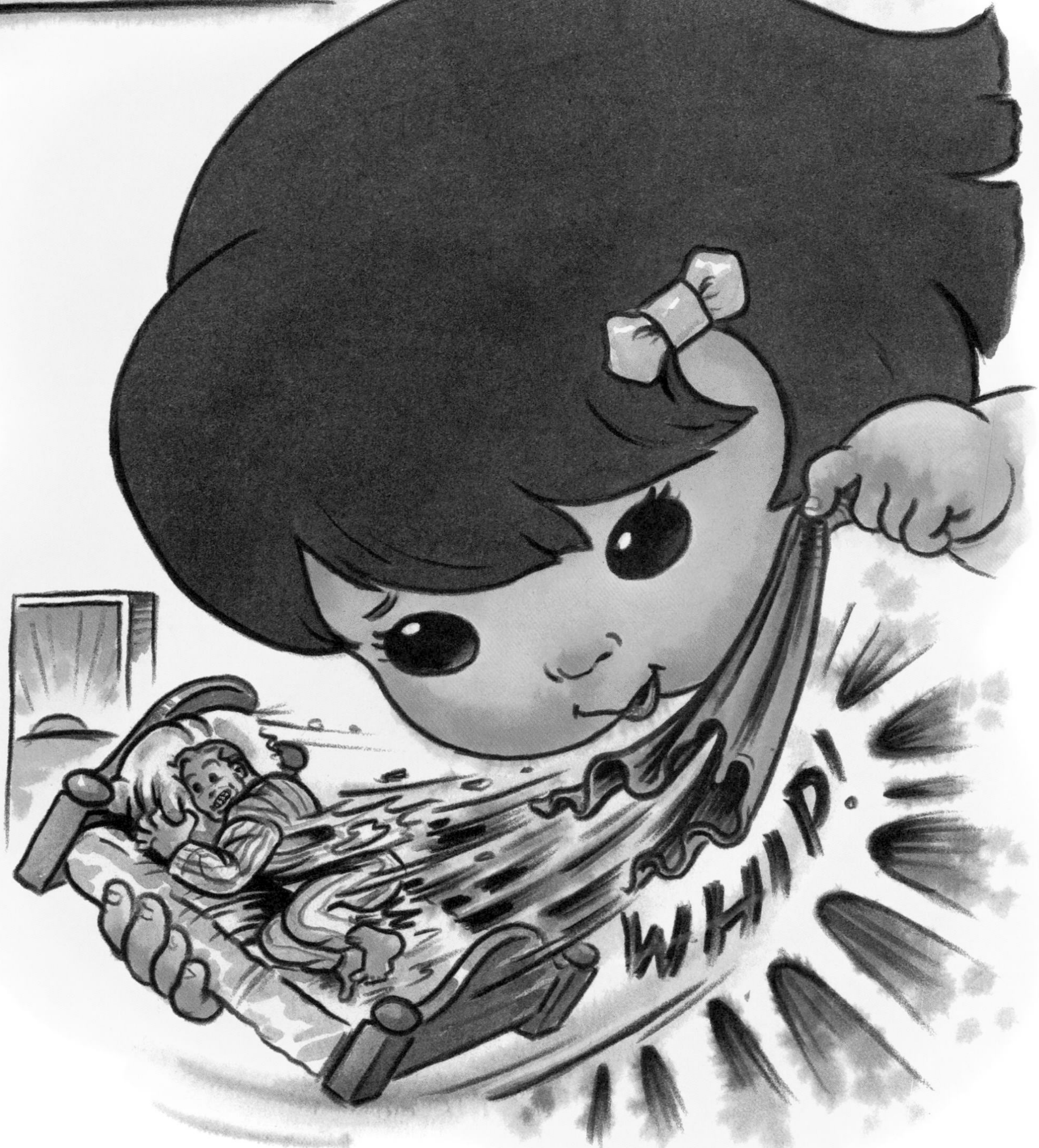
WHIP!

And being with her all through the long, long day . . .

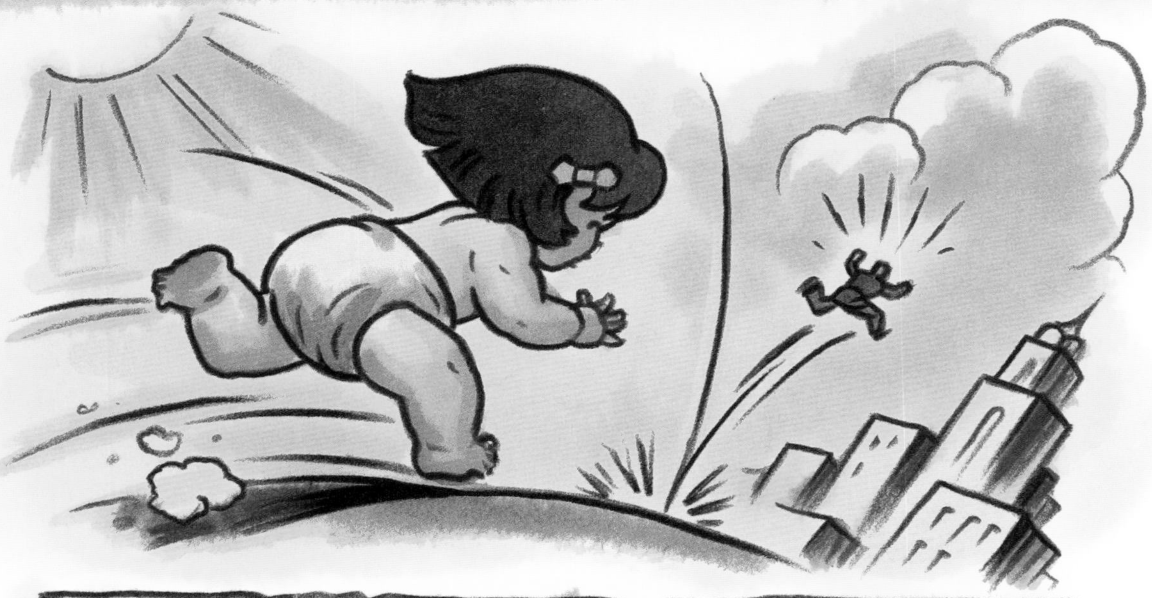

but the thing he loved MOST . . .

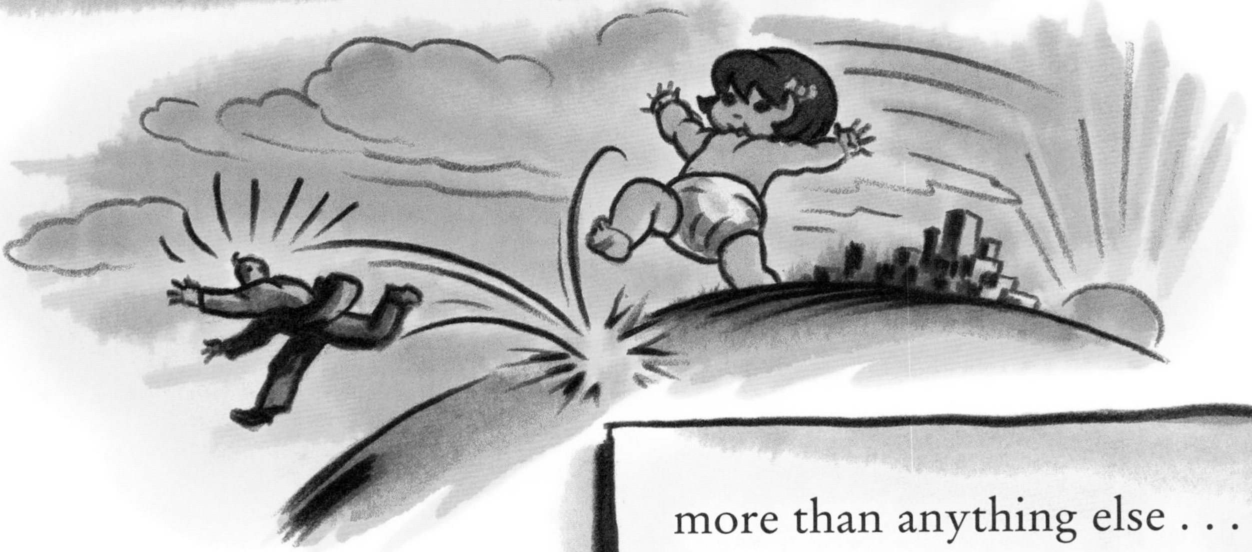

more than anything else . . .

Was watching her sleep!

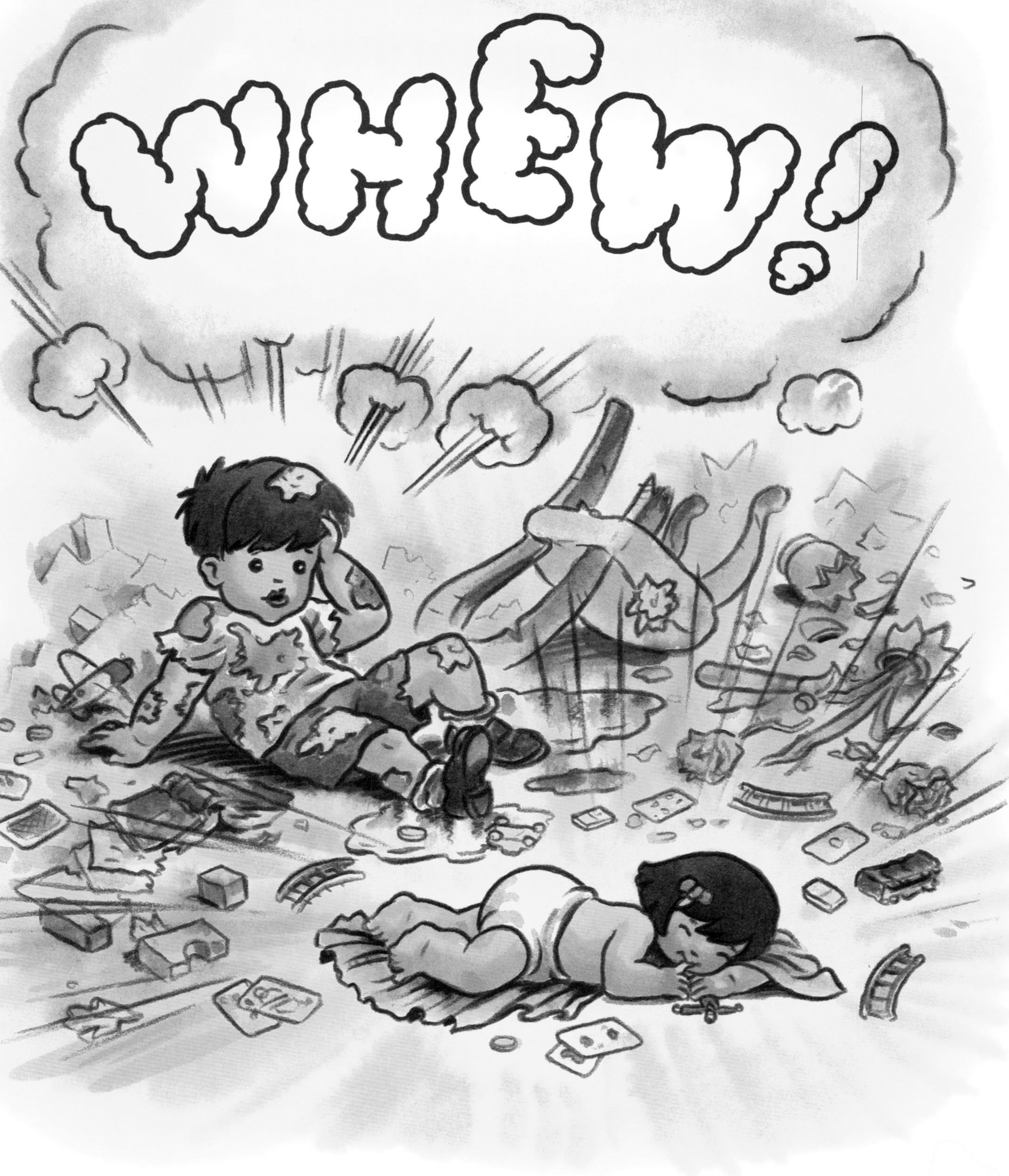
WHEW!